GHOSTS, LEGENDS, MYTHS
SAINT AUGUSTINE, FLORIDA
NATION'S OLDEST CITY

RANDY CRIBBS

RIVER PRESS, LLC ST AUGUSTINE, FLORIDA
WWW.RANDYCRIBBSAUTHOR.COM

Ghosts, Legends, and Myths
St. Augustine

Copyright 2020 by Randy Cribbs

LCCN: 2019919894

ISBN: 978-0-9849909-1-7

Published by River Press, LLC

Printed in the United States of America

Cover and illustrations by Ray Brilli

www.Raybrilliart.com

Cover and interior layout by Capri Porter

To obtain books go to www.randycribbsauthor.com; www.amazon.com; www.bn.com

Or write River Press, LLC 52 Tuscan Way Suite 202, #404, St Augustine, FL 32092

Author's Note

In 1565, Pedro Menendez de Aviles, Spain's most experienced Admiral, founded Saint Augustine. When the pilgrims subsequently came ashore at Plymouth, Saint Augustine was already a town with a fort, church, seminary, hospital, fish market and about 120 shops and houses.

It is indeed the nation's oldest city ... and host to restless spirits.

Randy Cribbs

About the Author

Randy Cribbs is a native of Florida; a retired U.S. Army officer and Vietnam veteran, he lives and writes in St Augustine. Randy holds degrees from the University of Florida, Pacific Lutheran University, Jacksonville State University, and is a graduate of the FBI National Academy and Armed Forces Staff College.

Since retiring from the Army, he has written twelve books, eight of which are set in St. Augustine.

Included among his several awards, two FWA Royal Palm Literary Best Book Awards, two FPA President's best book awards, and one FPA Silver Medal as well as a Moonbeam Young Adult Horror/mystery Silver Medal. His books have also been finalists in the Eric Hoffer and da Vinci Book Awards.

More information may be viewed at www.randycribbsauthor.com; www.bn.com; and www.amazon.com.

Books by Randy Cribbs

Were you there? Vietnam Notes

Tales from the Oldest City

One Summer in the Old Town

Illumination Rounds

The Vessel …Tinaja: An Ancient City Mystery

Ancient City Treasures

Ghosts: Another Summer in the Old Town

Just a Dog and the Musings of his Pet

Everything Is

Old St Augustine Through the Centuries

Color Me History – St. Augustine

Ghosts, Legends, and Myths: St. Augustine

**For more information go to:
www.randycribbsauthor.com**

About the Illustrator

Ray Brilli is a multiple award-winning artist who resides in Florida. He received his art education in New York city at the HS of Visual Arts, Hunter College, and School of Visual Arts. He has been a graphic designer for several Fortune 500 companies in New York City. His art is well known throughout Florida and beyond. www.Raybrilli-art.com

Dedicated To:

Anna Jane, Eilis, and Leah for those cold, dark, nights around the fire.

Table of Contents

Introduction

Ghosts have been haunting the earth since the beginning of mankind. A bold statement, but I make it because stories were told and passed on even before there were written records. It seems to me that as time passed and man began contemplating -- the unknown, the unexplained, events defying logic or explanation -- ghost stories became almost commonplace in virtually all cultures.

Indeed, ghosts have apparently been among us forever; we ponder the nature of friends and family members departed, visions or dreams, real or imagined, spirits both good and evil, strange appearances seen or felt. Whether one chooses to believe is a personal matter; unless of course you have experienced "something" that cannot be explained. Then your choice is somewhat dictated.

One of my novels revolves around ghosts, and since its publication years ago, I cannot begin to accurately state the number of times I have been asked: "Do you believe in ghosts?" I usually reply, "Do you?" Most of the time this response elicits a story, or at least an 'I heard ...'

Ghost stories run the gamut of good and

evil. Because ghosts seem to act in different ways, it has been suggested that ghost actions may be based on the observer and their subsequent reaction. Are they afraid, curious, accepting, skeptical? How one treats ghosts may be reciprocal. An old Eskimo wiseman said that "Only some can open the mind to all that is hidden to others."

Many readers seem to enjoy those stories not intended for the squeamish or faint of heart. Others prefer more kindly ghosts. These readers, as well as readers of the other genres who read short stories have at least one thing in common that draws them to the ghost tales. The unknown, the unexplainable, the curiosity of considering the stories validity or fantasy.

Most of the stories here have been told to us "natives" for generations. Many were told to me by folks whom I met through author appearances. Still others presented here were told by my wife's grandfather, Alfred Mosley, AKA" Honey man" who came to the Saint Augustine area as a young boy in the late 1800s. Some stories were told to him by friends in the nation's most haunted city, and some were based on events he either experienced or had first-hand knowledge.

Whether you choose to read ghost stories with lights burning brightly and windows secured firmly, or candles burning, curtains fluttering, perhaps rain dripping on the roof, enjoy!

Chapter One
Drake's Musician

To a reader of mysteries, final evaluation of a story's worth comes when the mystery is solved. A story that leaves the reader without a resolution or is lacking enough information for the reader themselves to resolve, can be exasperating. With ghosts, other world happenings, the mystery is usually unsolvable. The reader must accept that nothing can be proved or disproved unless the reader has also experienced the event presented.

On occasion, we all doubt our senses, particularly seeing and hearing. Why then would we not doubt the senses of those revealing impossible sights or sounds - those without plausible explanations? One reason to lessen doubt is the reporting of similar events over long periods of time from different people. This does not provide a solution, but it does lend some degree of credibility.

Downtown in the Old Town, many unusual things have been seen and heard. Probably much more than we know because many events are experienced by tourists who shortly leave, and their experiences are shared with others back home but not with those here. What one may hear during the daytime hustle and bustle of downtown, the noise of traffic and the drone of tour guides, is very different than that experienced on late evening walks or in the early hours of morning before disturbing commotion begins.

In the Old Town, among those things consistently reported over the years, is the faint, lilting sound of a flute or similar instrument. This seems to occur about halfway down Saint George Street near the center. The exact area is hard to isolate because the sound is barely audible, and the level doesn't change, louder or softer, as one searches for the source. It is described as "just being in the air, surrounding one".

Enough musical notes have been gleaned to say that it is almost certainly an organized tune, but to date not identified by anyone.

A young lad who worked at the Tradewinds Lounge, responsible for closing, routinely walked home down Saint George street between two and three o'clock in the morning. He relates hearing the sound and discounted that it could have come from any building because it was 'higher' in the air. His sister played the flute in years past, and he described the sound as something like that, but not exactly.

Some have linked these curious occurrences with a famous event that occurred here in 1586; Drake's Raid.

Drake was a very successful 'privateer', the official political term for a nation sponsored pirate. He raided under the English flag and his primary pickings came from Spanish held Caribbean cities and key ports as well as their bounty laden ships. He was so successful striking England's enemy and providing loot to the Crown that Queen Elizabeth I knighted him Sir Francis Drake.

Drake was headed home after pillaging several Spanish Caribbean ports and spotted a makeshift watchtower on Anastasia island across the inlet from the town. At that time, Saint Augustine was not much of a town, it had just over 300 residents, including about 150 Spanish soldiers. The town was only about eight city blocks that contained a few wooden buildings. The fort was under construction and was also wood. It did have 14 cannons. The town was commanded by the nephew of Saint Augustine's founder Pedro Menendez de Aviles. Compared to Drake's forces the town was a sitting duck, and in Drake's mind an easy quick target.

Drake landed a force on Anastasia island, but the small contingent he sent across the river was repelled by the fort's cannons. Since his ships could not enter the shallow water of the harbor, he decided to make a classic frontal assault with his soldiers.

Menendez, with the help of local Indians, made a surprise raid against Drake and inflicted several casualties. Menendez withdrew back to the fort where he shelled the intruders all night with cannon fire. He realized he was helplessly outnumbered, so he abandoned the fort and evacuated the town.

Preparing for their assault the next morning, the English heard the sound of a fife floating across the water. The song being played was an anti-Spanish tune known to all Protestants, the "Prince of Orange March". The musician was Nicholas Borgoignon, a French prisoner who had been captured by the Spanish at Fort Caroline several years earlier. During the evacuation he had escaped and was now alerting the English, by way of the tune, that the coast was clear.

The English mounted an immediate raid but discovered the now deserted town had been stripped bare by the evacuees. In their haste to leave, the Spanish did leave a chest containing a year's pay in support money for the soldiers and town, so Drake's Raid yielded some loot.

Drake decided to remain in the town for a few days so his men could rest and trade with the Indians. During this time his trusted second in command and loyal friend was killed by a sniper. This so enraged Drake that he ordered any remaining residents and the town destroyed. Every building was burned, the crops destroyed, and even the orange grove that had been started by the Spanish was cut down. Unintentionally, Drake's ally, the French musician was killed by a stray musket ball.

This disastrous raid was almost the end of Saint Augustine because many in Spain wanted to abandon the settlement. This was avoided when several military and naval notables convinced King Phillip of its military and strategic importance. It took several years to rebuild and fortify the Old Town.

During the following centuries in the Old Town, reports of lilting, haunting music have persisted. Could it be the described flute like music sometimes heard is a fife being played by the ghost of the French prisoner Nicholas Borgoignon?

It is impossible to know for certain, but apparently, something or someone continues to play a tune on a flute or fife, heard only when it's very quiet.

You're invited to take an early morning or late evening stroll on St George Street. Perhaps you'll be able to identify the haunting tune and solve the mystery. Surely someone will, eventually?

Chapter Two
The House

Several years ago, I asked a dear friend of mine to review the manuscript of my newest book, a ghost mystery. Jim was a popular, widely published author who was several years my senior. We had met and become close friends many years earlier. Jim didn't write much anymore, but he seemed to enjoy reviewing the work of others and had always provided very helpful comments on my work.

A few days later Jim called, said he had finished reviewing my manuscript and suggested lunch for the following day on Saint George Street. Of course, I agreed, insisting that it would be my treat as a reward for his labor -- a joke we had come to share since Jim would never accept payment for his work.

After we had placed our order, Jim handed me the manuscript, and I could see some of his scrawled margin notes. He stated that he enjoyed the story and as always, I could do with his comments whatever I chose. He took a sip of water and asked if he had ever told me his haunted house story. He had not, but I urged him to do so now.

In the 1950s, Jim, then a budding but already popular Saint Augustine author, befriended a newcomer to town, a man we'll call Tyson, who had relocated here and started a printing business. He also speculated with properties, and his recent purchase was a very old, large two-story house that had been unoccupied for years and was in need of repair. This house was located directly behind the center of Saint George Street.

Not sure how he would renovate the house, either rental rooms or as a single dwelling, he decided to clean it up and rent some of the rooms to workers in the downtown area until he had a more definitive plan.

The rooms rented quickly but no one would stay, claiming that no one could live there because the house was weird, creepy, even possessed! The word got out, and soon there were no tenants. Someone told him about a woman nearby who had fallen on hard times and might be willing to stay there if the price was cheap enough. Tyson let her stay for free because he needed to put the haunting gossip to rest, and she would keep things in order, airing out some rooms, dusting, and so on. This arrangement worked well for several weeks, until the lady was found dead in her bed. The cause of death could not be determined, but it was said her facial expression in death was one of horror. Predictably, this further perpetuated the many stories about the house.

Jim, somewhat an adventurous type and with the natural curiosity of a writer, suggested the two of them spend the night in the house. Jim would then pen an article for the local paper debunking the ghost gossip. He added jokingly that he would bring his dog Bogart to protect them. It was agreed and the date was selected, allowing some time for the word to get out.

Jim decided to track down a couple of the people who had rented rooms, though briefly. One didn't want to talk about it, and the other, a young lad who worked on Saint George Street, was not very helpful. He said only that it was not so much what was seen or heard that drove him out, but rather an undeniable terror that would seize him. Apparently, this happened primarily when passing certain rooms in which no one resided or could be seen. He told Jim which rooms.

The appointed day arrived, and the two men met at the house. Jim brought his dog Bogart as promised, and a pistol, though he did not reveal this to Tyson. It was to be an unusual chilly summer night, somewhat overcast, but still there would be a moon, shining brighter as clouds dissipated later.

When the two men were in the entry hall, the door closed behind them and Bogart, who had run in eagerly, went back to the door, scratching and whining to get out. Jim reassured the animal who, resigned to not being let out, followed close on Jim's heels. This struck Jim as odd because the dog's normal behavior would have been darting about, sniffing new areas.

They decided to get a fire going in the large, old fireplace to take the chill off. They then walked around visiting the various downstairs rooms and kitchen where they discovered two bottles of cobweb covered wine. Tyson commented that apparently ghosts didn't drink. They stepped outside into the backyard which was bordered with a high brick wall but avoided the steppingstones which were damp and covered with growth.

As they turned to re-enter the house, Jim could see before him on the stone path the impression of a footprint being made. In front of it, another appeared. This continued until the backdoor steps were reached. Needless to say, this aroused Jim's curiosity, but very much bothered Tyson.

They returned to the front room where there was now a nice fire. As they were about to sit in two of the old armchairs, another chair moved noiselessly from the other wall and came to rest in front of Jim. Jim swore that as he watched, the dim outline of a human figure appeared in the chair. It was so dim, he wondered if he could trust his vision.

Jim got up and moved the chair back to the far wall while Tyson stared without moving. Jim set the chair down, and as he raised up, something touched him on the shoulder, sharply. He jerked around thinking it was Tyson, but he was still seated. Tyson also appeared frightened, so Jim did not mention the incident.

They sat for a short while enjoying the fire. Remembering the task at hand, Jim suggested they check the other rooms. Tyson agreed but not with enthusiasm. Jim tried to open the door of a room just off the front room. It was either stuck or locked. As Tyson fumbled with a large ring of keys he had brought, the door slowly opened. Exchanging glances, they entered.

The room was almost empty except for a few empty boxes scattered about. As they turned to exit, the door by which they had entered closed quietly. Now Jim was beginning to get a little uneasy. Tyson was almost in shock. He grabbed the doorknob and jerked on the door forcibly. It did not budge. Jim directed Tyson to stand back. He then kicked the door several times with all the force he could muster. Nothing. Cold air surrounded them. Their breath could be seen as on a cold morning. Now they were both feeling something akin to horror. Jim prepared to kick the door again, but before he could, it slowly opened.

They scurried into the hall, relieved that the ordeal was over. They turned and something to their right front caught their attention. A large pale light, the size of a human figure but more shapeless, began to form. It ascended the stairs.

Heart pounding, Jim followed. Tyson hesitated, then started up behind him. A door opened to one of the rooms and the apparition entered. The light floated to an old bed and seemed to collapse into a smaller form, quivered, and vanished. They approached and examined the old dusty bed but found nothing out of the ordinary.

There was a small book on the dusty nightstand, Jim picked it up and then heard footsteps. They exchanged worried glances as the footsteps' sound headed out the door. They followed the soft sounds as they descended the stairs. About halfway down, the footsteps stopped, and Jim felt something tugging on the book he had secured. He increased his hold and the effort stopped.

The two men returned to the chairs and fireplace. Jim set the pistol on a small table next to him. Tyson had sat down, then decided to search for a bathroom. Shortly after, a loud knocking could be heard, but it was difficult to determine from where. Bogart sat up, ears twitching. He rose, still staring at Jim with a wild stare, hair brisling. Suddenly Tyson reappeared with a look of pure horror on his face. Without speaking, he made for the door, opened it and headed down the street. Jim ran through the open door and called to him, but Tyson never looked back. Jim re- entered the house, but before he could close the door it slammed shut. Jim's first thought was that he should follow Tyson. His curiosity would not let him. He resolved to see the process through. He retrieved his pistol from the table and headed for a nearby bedroom, a smaller one he had noted earlier. Its size would hopefully offer a sense of security, true or not.

He entered the room, Bogart on his heels, shut and locked the door. Bogart went immediately to a corner, obviously terrified. He kept snarling and showing his teeth, all the while staring at Jim, who was afraid to console him for fear of getting bitten because the poor animal was in such a state.

Jim stretched out on the bed, determined to ride things out. He turned on the small dimly lit lamp next to the bed. It only cast light two or three feet. He sat the pistol down and reached for the book he had set on the table by the lamp. A shadow fell across the old worn cover. He jerked his head around and could see across the small room, in the semidarkness, an undefined outline. Whether or not it was human form, he could not tell. It seemed gigantic, the top of it almost touching the ceiling.

Jim became aware that it had gotten extremely cold. It seemed he could barely see two eyes, or at least pale light where eyes should be. He reached for the pistol and felt his arm being struck. Then suddenly, the lamp went out and the room was in total darkness.

Jim felt powerless. Determined not to lay in the dark at the mercy of what lurked within, he leaped from the bed and ran to the one window, throwing open the curtains. The moon had finally freed itself of clouds and offered at least some light.

He moved quickly to the nightstand where he snatched the pistol. he reflected humorously that he wasn't sure what good it would do against something he assumed was not among the living. In any event, it caused him to feel more secure, or at least less insecure. The large, shadowy glob was now very dim. He decided to make for the door and as an afterthought, grabbed the book. Something resisted and he could see another, smaller, shadowy form. He wrestled the book free and now could hear loud footsteps outside the door. The two shadows changed into bluish lights as the steps grew louder, as if moving closer. The door of an old wardrobe closet flew open so violently, it sounded as if the hinges had broken free.

Jim ran to the door, hoping it would open but afraid of what he would find on the other side. The knob and bolt latch burned his hands. He yelled, but through the flash of pain got the door open. The footsteps stopped, but another dim figure moved through his body into the room, momentarily leaving him breathless.

He bolted through the door and turned. The new arrival had also turned from shadow to a bluish white light and all three visitors moved toward each other to the sound of low murmuring. The murmuring grew louder, and the entire room seemed to vibrate. The three lights grew brighter and almost animated, as if a fight had ensued.

Suddenly one light briefly took shape and seemed to enter a wall where it disappeared. The murmuring had stopped, and Jim watched as the other two lights seemed to blend and merge into one. Everything grew quiet. Jim hurried back to the front room where Bogart awaited him, having darted out of the bedroom in the commotion without being seen. He immediately ran to the front door and began scratching at it.

The dog's action caused him to realize that the primary goal and reason for his presence had not been accomplished. Neither was there a reason to continue any part of it; debunking ghosts in the house could not be done. As far as he was concerned, quite the opposite had been proven. Bogart darted out before Jim could get the door fully open. He ran down the steps into the far end of the yard where he watched for his master. Jim shut the door, not bothering to lock it and joined the animal. He picked Bogart up to reassure him and headed home.

Tyson called the next day, ashamed and apologetic. Jim assured him it was not a problem, and in fact told Tyson he had chosen the right course of action. Jim asked him what he thought his plans for the house might be now. Tyson responded that he was not sure, but he definitely would not be renting it! Jim also asked what he knew about the history of the house. Tyson reported not much, other than its age and the fact that after the original owners, it changed hands frequently, a condition they could both understand!

A few days passed as Jim tried to reconcile what they had experienced. He remembered the old book he had found and upon untying its leather strap, discovered it was a diary, or journal. As he read through it, it became obvious the writer was a woman, possibly one of the first residents of the house based on the few pages dated. The picture of a young man fell out, he was handsome, thirties, with the huge swooping mustache of the 1800s era. On the back was written the words "until we are together".

Jim also gathered from the diary that the woman's husband was reasonably affluent and traveled often. Many sections seem to imply he was also abusive, neglectful, and jealous. But was the picture her husband? Jim was skeptical because the writer referred often to a "H" in somewhat coded fashion. This could have been a protective measure in case her book was discovered. Jim's curiosity greatly aroused, he decided to research the house and hopefully discover information that might explain the strange events.   After days of searching old newspaper files and talking to several old residents who were alive during the era in question, Jim put together what he thought was the situation.

The original owner of the house was Artemis Rafferty who presented himself as a man of means. He gained a reputation as a gambler, womanizer, and a man to do business with only if necessary. He took a young wife in town, Rachel, who was from a family of modest means and apparently married Artemis against her father's wishes. It was soon widely known that Artemis was indeed abusive to the girl.

Artemis traveled often and, in her loneliness, Rachel befriended a young man, Harold, who delivered goods from the local general store. It was generally thought that their relationship was that of friends, though obviously their feelings ran deeper. Jim related that the mother of an old timer he talked to said that Harold frequently consoled the girl after her husband's abuse.

A series of old newspaper stories revealed that Artemis returned home from a trip to find Harold, who had just brought a store delivery, having lemonade with Rachel in the backyard. Artemis began calling her names and struck her. Harold took exception and grabbed the outraged husband, at which time Artemis pulled a derringer a shot Harold dead. Artemis was arrested but soon released, no doubt due in part to the era of husband's rights and so on. The newspaper picture of the deceased was the young man in the diary photo.

Artemis's treatment of Rachel became more severe and during one of his drunken beatings of the girl, she grabbed a shotgun and killed him. Just prior, neighbors reported a great deal of fighting and yelling, that, combined with Rachel's many bruises, suggested self-defense was the reason for her also not being charged. Nevertheless, a few weeks later she killed herself.

Jim grew quiet and I realized he had finished his story. I asked him what happened to the house. He said Tyson tore it down and sold the property. I asked Jim what street was this house on, but he replied he had promised Tyson he would never tell the exact location. I commented that the story would make a hell of a book. He laughed and said he was going to do that a few years later, but every time he started, he couldn't seem to focus. To my question of why he thought that was, he said he wasn't certain because he had written several other books since. Then, he reflected, smiled and said simply that maybe it has something to do with my strong intuition I should "let these ghosts lie".

Chapter Three

Lily

Saint Francis Inn was built during the second Spanish period, about 1791. For many years, it has been one of the most popular bed and breakfast Inns in the Old Town. Over the years, there have been so many reports of sightings and unusual happenings at the Inn, it is impossible to put a number on the events.

The Inn has been the subject of national television programs and has been visited by paranormal investigators, most of whom reported readings on their various meters that were off the charts. On a personal note, for several years I have been a guest author at the annual bed and breakfast tour held at the Inn. During that time, I have met previous guests who have experienced something while staying at the Inn. To me, that fact certainly lends some credibility to the stories I have heard many times. Most seem to be centered around one room and one person, Lily. Whether or not Lily was the name of the person in question I cannot say, but her spirit has become known as Lily, and the room is 3 A.

In the early to mid-nineteenth century,

the house was occupied by a military officer, his family, and a nephew who lived with them. The nephew fell in love with a young servant girl who worked for the family and before long, they were secretly meeting in the third-floor attic, today's room 3 A.

When the uncle discovered them, he had his nephew, a soldier, posted to a faraway location. The reason the nephew was sent away is speculated to be because Lily was a valuable servant to the uncle, and he didn't want to lose her. When the nephew finally returned years later, Lily, was no longer there. Whether or not she died or just left is unclear. In any event, the nephew, heartbroken, could not recover and finally took his own life.

I need to point out here that there are at least two other versions concerning how the lovers died. One has the nephew hanging himself in the attic or jumping from the attic window to his death. Another suggests it was Lily who hung herself and her lover subsequently did likewise. Exact circumstances will no doubt remain unclear, but it does appear that both still frequent the Inn.

There have been consistent reports of guests and staff members seeing a young girl in 19th century dress, usually in the room, but sometimes the hallway. Occasionally, guests have reported hearing a young girl's voice. Some visitors have awakened to find personal possessions in disarray, particularly ladies' jewelry. It was known that Lily enjoyed jewelry and having none of her own, made a habit of trying on the trinkets of others. While guests have never reported jewelry missing, many have suggested that their personal trinkets appeared to have been moved around.

On one occasion, a woman in the room awoke to a passionate kiss, only to find her husband fast asleep.

Many of the staff reported that often the aroma of pipe smoke was smelled. It was known that the nephew was fond of his pipe. Smoking has not been allowed on the premises for years, so guests' smoking would not account for the occasional smell.

A longtime employee of the Inn told me that a contractor working at the Inn commented on a lady working upstairs and asked if she was a new employee. There were no new employees, and when the upstairs was checked, no one was present. This person also told me that she witnessed at least three instances of movement in 3A: a short window curtain began fluttering for no apparent reason; a small lamp flickered on and off; and the bed cover moved on its own.

Sightings of Lily persist. Apparently, several guests making reservations at the Inn have asked for Lily's room, with the obvious expectation of meeting her. Most do not, but those who do, are excited by their encounter, and often re-book Lily's room for their next visit.

Chapter Four

Garden Lovers

Among those who study afterlife encounters are those who believe ghosts act in different ways based on the person encountering them and their subsequent reaction to those ghosts. Are they afraid, curious, aggressive, accepting? How one "treats" their ghost may be reciprocal!

A large two story, well-appointed house on Carrera street is said to have occasional backyard strollers, usually described as a young couple.

The house, built around 1900, still stands, though renovated several times. It was designed and first occupied by a family of means from the northeast who vacationed in Saint Augustine and decided to move there permanently. The wealthy businessman, his wife, and 18-year-old daughter, Sybil, soon moved in the highest city social circles and were very influential.

Sybil and her mother installed a beautiful backyard garden of flowers, shrubs, and a system of small stone pathways, weaving among many varieties of plants and flowers, including a unique trellis, covered with wild, sweet smelling roses with a swing where one could pause to enjoy the fragrance. This became Sybil's favorite place. She would sit for hours enjoying the garden and soft coastal breeze.

The young lady's father was very protective and paid close attention to suitors who wished to call on Sybil. If they did not meet the father's expectations, or their station in life was not high enough, they were sent packing.

Sybil was in no hurry to marry and patiently tolerated this situation; until Robert showed up.

Robert worked for the fellow who was hired to keep the garden well appointed. He shared Sybil's love of plants and flowers, and they would talk while he tended his backyard chores. They soon realized their feelings for each other went far deeper than a common love for flowers. So did her father.

Alarmed at her obvious infatuation with this 'commoner', Sybil's father had the lad fired and forbade her ever seeing him again. He then set about providing the 'proper suitors' to call. Sybil, given no choice in the matter went along, though she did make it clear, in a gracious way, that she was not interested.

Her parents' bedroom was located on the front side of the house which made it convenient to meet Robert in the garden after her parents retired for the night. This arrangement continued until one of her father's arranged suitors, Percy, discovered Sybil's feelings for Robert.

Having decided that he was the one for Sybil, Percy went to the town stables, where Robert now worked, to confront him. Robert told Percy that he loved Sybil and she him and that it was Percy who should break it off. The argument quickly escalated into a physical confrontation resulting in Percy being knocked into a pitchfork and killed.

Robert knew he stood no chance coming out of this situation alive, given the influence of both Percy's and Sybil's fathers, so he ran, after first sending word to Sybil that he would return for her. The manhunt was unsuccessful. Some said Robert was hiding in the swamps near the Saint Johns River, others had him in Georgia. In any event, he could not be found, much to the sheriff's embarrassment.

Sybil was broken hearted. She would not attend any social gatherings, wanting only to stroll the garden; her and Robert's garden. Months passed, and she became more heartbroken. She grew more and more weak, until finally, she died.

Within weeks after Sybil's death, Robert surreptitiously returned to take her away, but upon discovering she had passed, he gave himself up to the sheriff, who at the urging of the influential fathers and, with little fanfare, hung him at the old jail.

As time passed, Sybil's mother began telling her no nonsense husband that she saw Sybil in the garden. This became more frequent and fearing for his wife's sanity, he sold the house and they moved further south.

The house was bought by a middle age couple unfamiliar with the events concerning Sybil and Robert and the garden. This soon changed when the wife woke her husband up one night to tell him someone was in the backyard. He grabbed his gun and a light but could find no evidence of intruders.

This happened several times over the course of several months with no trespassers found, but the wife insisting she had seen two figures. The husband asked a neighbor if he had any problem with prowlers. The neighbor said no but told him the story about the killing and deaths of the two lovers. He added that the girls' mother was certain that Sybil and Robert continued to visit the garden.

The new owner, tired of being awakened by his wife and given reports of ghosts, decided to move to Anastasia Island and make this house a rental.

For the next few years, the house had many tenants and many recurring complaints to the owner about people seen in the backyard at night. The hired gardener also reported to the owner that on occasion, he would show up to work the garden, only to find that it had already been trimmed.

Having had enough, the owner, a patriotic fellow, sold the house at an unbelievable deal to a widow whose husband had been killed in World War II a few years earlier. Mrs. Kirk moved in and lived in the house for 50 plus years. Her ten-year-old son, John, grew up in the house and lived with her until he finished school and started a law practice in Saint Augustine. It is from John that the rest of this story comes.

After they had been in the house about one year, Mrs. Kirk awoke late one night for no explicable reason other than an unusual feeling. She decided to go check on her son, whose room was on the backside of the house, overlooking the garden.

John was sleeping soundly. A very bright moon was shining through the large window and a breeze was causing the curtains to flutter. As she put her hands on the window to lower it, she glanced out over her beautiful garden and saw two barely discernible figures who seemed to be gazing up at her. As she stared, the figures became more recognizable as a young woman in a long flowing dress, such as a fashionable young lady would wear and beside her a young man in an old modest suit.

Mrs. Kirk raised the window higher so she

would not be encumbered by the curtains and stuck her head out so she could better see. To her amazement, the couple walked around the trellis and sat down in the swing. It began swinging gently.

She pulled her head back inside and rubbed her sleep filled eyes and peered through the opening again. She watched, unafraid, but mesmerized as the couple slowly disappeared, leaving the swing gently moving for a few moments.

Thinking her sleep fogged mind was playing tricks on her, she closed the window and returned to her bed.

She had a similar experience a few days later, suggesting the first time had not been her imagination.

Curious, she began making inquiries about the history of the house and discovered the story about Sybil and Robert.

John said his Mom was convinced the couple she saw was indeed Sybil and Robert. She frequently stayed up late to see if they would appear; many times, they did. Sometimes not. It was not long before John experienced the couple himself.

One night, John woke his Mom to report that someone was in the backyard. She accompanied him back to his bedroom and looking out the window, saw the couple looking back.

Mrs. Kirk, an educated, independent woman, was not given to fantasies or illogical pursuits. She raised her son to be that way; open minded, not prejudiced. Now, she decided to share her honest thoughts on this matter, with no deception.

John listened, then went to the window and waved. To his amazement, the young lady waved back. John was no longer scared and in fact could not contain his excitement. Mrs. Kirk thought it prudent to suggest he not tell his friends about their ghosts just yet, explaining the possible consequences. He agreed and kept that secret well until his later years when he confided to a friend. He laughed at the time and told his friend that when friends or relatives were visiting and would comment on movement in the yard, he would attribute it to the wind. He also told his friend that frequently, his Mom would leave cookies and tea on a stand beside the swing, but they were never eaten. When he pointed out this fact to his Mom, she just said that ghosts probably don't need to eat, but she just wanted them to know they were welcome.

Chapter Five
Old Jail

Several years ago, there was quite a com-motion late one night when several fire trucks and the police responded to a frantic call from a tourist couple who reported a fire in the old jail and someone moving around inside. The jail had been closed for several hours, and a thorough search revealed neither a fire, nor anyone on the premises.

The tourists, a retired policeman and his wife, insisted they had seen what they reported! After calling 911, he had banged on the jail door trying to get the person's attention while his wife kept track of the person moving inside. She only lost sight of the person when the fire trucks ar-rived. They would not leave until the authorities allowed them to enter the jail and see for them-selves that there wasn't a fire or victim inside. Strange event, but then the Old Jail has a history of strange happenings.

There is a wonderful older neighborhood directly behind the jail, and many of the resi-dents there enjoy evening walks along the qui-et streets, one of which lies directly behind the building. For years, there have been plentiful stories regarding the reports of these folks and in fact others, seeing or hearing unusual things as they strolled by.

The sound of low singing has been heard, as well as the murmuring of several voices. The trap door of the gallows, approximately 40 feet from the street has been heard dropping open.

The jail opened in 1891 and was quite a structure for its time, boasting two-foot-thick cement walls and a state of the art lock up system. The sheriff's family quarters were located at the south end of the building and were well appointed. All this was made possible by the generosity, or perhaps more correctly the insistence of Henry Flagler.

His famous Ponce de Leon Hotel, now Flagler College, had been built and was thriving...the lodging of choice for the wealthy northerners flocking to Saint Augustine. At that time, the local jail was located very near the hotel. No doubt out of respect and concern for his affluent guests, Flagler did not like this arrangement. He offered to buy land and build a new jail if the city leaders agreed to locate it further out of downtown. Of course, they agreed.

Flagler really didn't spare much expense for the effort. The inside, though lacking in frills, such as glass windows, heat, and other amenities was modern as jails go.

The outside, however was different. Queen

Anne style architecture with Victorian brickwork. It was one of Saint Augustine's more beautiful buildings and was frequently thought to be an attractive hotel by visitors entering town. Flagler's fine building design was done because most of his hotel visitors passed by the jail on their way to his place, and he wanted to ensure they got a favorable first impression of the town. Also, residents in the immediate area had to be happy, and they surely were.

Sheriff Joe Perry served as Sheriff for 26 years, from the opening of the new jail in 1891 until 1919, with a four-year absence during that time. He was a large man at six and a half feet tall and 300 pounds. He was also a bold man and was said to have gone with his deputies on the more dangerous calls. He ruled the prisoner population in a no-nonsense fashion and was a firm believer in discipline.

Felons sentenced to death were hung on the gallows behind the jail. It was reported that one prisoner was hung, cut down and taken to the isolation cell as was the rule, until the body could be claimed. In this case however, the man regained consciousness and had to be hung again. It has been said by some that he has been seen on occasion around the gallows.

The jail is known as one of the most haunted buildings in the county. It has been visited by dozens of teams specializing in paranormal events; many of whom reported unusual findings. Mediums and psychics have particularly reported positive experiences. Strange events have also been reported by tourists, residents and employees.

Apparitions have been seen on occasion but, more frequently, occurrences are less defined: the sense that you're being watched; a slight movement when no one else is around; shadows where none should be ; all manner of noises such as footsteps, low singing, moans, and of course, chains rattling. For the most part it is employees who experience these occurrences, probably because they're the ones in the building alone, when tourists are not present, talking, laughing -- generally being loud. Noise is not conducive to experiencing other "happenings". Many insist they smelled food cooking in the kitchen area.

On a personal note, when I was working on one of my other books: "Ghosts: Another Summer in the Old Town", I too, experienced "something." My book is a mystery that revolves around a mysterious link between the Old Jail and Tolomato Cemetery, so during my research I was allowed to tour the jail alone while it was deserted. It's a spooky place.

On the first occasion, my visit was somewhat hurried because a tour was about to start. My quick observations, primarily to get a sense of things, was almost uneventful, but not totally. I say this because you hear "things" in the old building. I reminded myself that there is a substantial amount of cement and steel in the structure and those building materials make noise as a result of weather, settling, and so on. Nevertheless, though hurried, I heard a variety of noises, most I believe, explainable.

My second visit was timed just at closing, so I would not be in such a hurry and was more interesting.

To start, upon entering I could have sworn I heard a low voice. I had been told no one else was in the jail. I checked and found I was indeed alone.

I stood for a moment at the base of the steps going up to the cells. I had an overpowering feeling of sadness. Perhaps sympathy for all those prisoners of yesteryear. I started up the steps and had the strong sensation I was being watched. I stopped and glanced around to find I was still alone.

As I reached the top landing, I clearly heard a scraping noise and stopped in mid stride. From behind me there was a slight sound like someone else was climbing the stairs and took one more step after I had stopped. There was, of course no one there.

I can't honestly say I wasn't concerned. During my entire visit, the air around me felt heavy: a feeling of smothering closeness, like a vacuum being created.

Although I enjoyed meeting all the great folks who work at the jail and learning the fascinating history tied to this place; I have no desire to tour the jail alone again!

Chapter Six

The Treasure of Indian Charles

Over a century ago, two enterprising young men from the college in Gainesville made the slow tedious trip east to the Saint Johns River near Saint Augustine. They had heard one could find indian artifacts, possibly burial mounds in the swampy areas off the river, favorite camp-sites of local indians long ago. Largely unregulated at that time, artifacts could be sold for a good profit.

They picked an area of the swamp based on an old faded map one of the men had purchased from a secondhand shop. Although the legitimacy of the map was unknown, they deducted the indians would have camped near the riverbank but more inland towards higher ground. They entered the swamp, excited about the prospects of picking up a few bucks.

After several hours of sloshing through the thick vegetation, they saw a small clearing and what appeared to be the remains of some type of wooden shelter, long abandoned. Thinking this a likely spot to start, it was agreed that one would set up their tent while the other probed the ground for likely digging areas.

The man erecting the tent had almost completed his task when he heard his friend yell. He turned to see him suspended in the air, parallel to the ground, being shook by something unseen. As his body was slung back and forth, blood spurting, his yells became louder. The yelling stopped as he took his last breath. The tent builder, frozen in place, could now make out two hideous eyes and the shape of something very large. The beast dropped his friend and was joined by another beast of equal size, both snarling. Behind the beasts, the young man could see the wavy image of a human figure, and then the beasts were on him! Neither of these young men were ever heard from again and the irony is that they were not even looking for the treasure the beasts were guarding. That's where the story really begins.

In the late 1800s, throughout southern and coastal Georgia, a string of robberies occurred. These continued over a couple of years and included banks, homes of the wealthy, and at least three thefts of large payrolls during transport.

This continued until the thief moved south into Jacksonville Florida and robbed the mansion of an extremely wealthy and powerful man. While he stole a large sum of cash, the gentleman victim was most outraged by the loss of a box of priceless gold coins he had collected for years. As sometimes is the case when the affluent and powerful are wronged, law enforcement throughout southern Georgia and north Florida became much more aggressive.

As various jurisdictions coordinated their hunt, the robberies stopped, and it became clear that not much was known about the culprit. Some reports described a large man with dark eyes and dark complexion; another noted that he wore a black hat with a beaded band into which a feather was stuck. Indian? Still three other witnesses stated that as the mysterious robber rode away on horseback, two very large dogs appeared and ran with him. One of these witnesses, newly arrived from the West, said they weren't dogs at all, they were wolves.

The robberies never started again, but word of the robber's exploits spread throughout the countryside.

In a time when news was scarce and slow, it became an item of much discussion when it finally did arrive.

Cutter's general store was located about 20 miles west of St Augustine FL along the banks of the Saint Johns River near Six Mile Creek. Cutter's was the place in this sparsely populated area to get maps, offer opinions, and, of course, discuss the latest news including the robber and especially the large reward offered for the missing box of gold coins.

Cutter, having the advantage of owning the store and being present constantly, was the recipient of all the news, stories and variations of stories that were told as people would come and go.

Being a curious fellow, Cutter pieced together bits and pieces of the robbers' exploits and descriptions and realized that a newcomer to the area fit at least part of the descriptions.

Though the newcomer had patronized the store only two or three times, it occurred to Cutter that the stranger, who seldom spoke, was a dark man, and on one occasion had dogs with him. During that visit he had tied his horse and left the dogs a considerable distance from the store, but Cutter could tell they were extremely large and indeed, appeared wolf like.

A few days after Cutter's revelation, the area's young constable stopped by the store. This young lad was well known, having grown up in the area. He was well thought of by the way he handled the various incidents that occurred in this rural area; too much moonshine, chicken theft, the occasional friendly fight.

As you might imagine, this young man's job was not the most exciting in the world, so his ears perked up when Cutter told him his observations concerning the stranger. What he could not tell the lad was the man's name, where he lived, or anything else.

Nevertheless, the constable thought it was worth looking into. As the constable made his rounds throughout the countryside over the following weeks, he was amazed at how little was known about the stranger presumably living in the area. That changed when he had to pay a visit to an old man who lived in the swamps of Jack Wright Island. The old man, Henry, who kept to himself, but was well known by all, had been accused of stealing another man's fish traps, in this area, a serious matter.

The alleged fish trap thief lived very near the riverbank in his swamp shack, so the constable decided to go by skiff. His surprise visit found Henry putting new rope on several fish traps which he vigorously claimed as his own. Since there was no evidence to prove otherwise, the constable partially accepted Henry's claim. But before leaving, he asked Henry if he was aware of the stranger. Hesitating, the old man said he might have seen him a time or two. The constable, excited that he might finally get information, offered a deal; if Henry would give his accuser some of the alleged stolen traps and tell what he knew about the stranger, there would be no further inquiry. The old man, who wanted to be left alone, agreed.

The stranger in question was named Charles and he lived much deeper in the swamps. Charles had approached the old man asking him where he could get a skiff. He wanted a way to get to the ferry landing at Picalota to catch a carriage into Saint Augustine for supplies.

Henry found him a skiff and was paid well in cash. He added that Charles might get upset that his location had been revealed because the suspect robber had paid him extra not to discuss their transaction or encounter. The constable assured him his secret was safe.

The young constable, convinced that Charles could well be the robber, started formulating a plan. He now knew Charles had a skiff and he was seen on horseback. The island was only accessible by shallow water skiff; unless you wanted to brave the Gators and moccasins for about one and a half miles through the wetland to an old logging road. Only those who had grown up in the area or had been in the area a long time could safely do that. Apparently, Charles could get to where he lived by both means. With this revelation, the constable felt certain he could find the suspected robber's camp. The constable enlisted Cutter and two other men as his posse. They took the old logging road and tied the horses at a point in the swamp just short of the suspected abode of Charles.

The men moved cautiously through the swamp until just ahead they could make out a crudely constructed cracker shack. As they neared the dwelling, the front door opened and two huge wild-eyed dogs jumped out and headed for the men, growling and snarling.

One of the beasts grabbed the lead man

by the arm. Cutter shot the other dog dead, then turned and shot the one ripping at his friend's arm. While this was happening, Charles was lunging at the constable, and before the young lad could pull his revolver, Charles stabbed him in the chest, killing him instantly. The third posse member who had been trailing the constable hit Charles with his shotgun stock, knocking him unconscious.

Several hours later, the men showed up at Cutter's store, with the constable draped over his horse. They reported that they had discovered the fugitive on the river, and there was a shootout resulting in the killing of the young constable. The fugitive was hit but managed to jump into the river and never came up. They figured he drowned, or a gator got him, or both.

The real story, told by the man whose arm was mangled by one of Charles' beasts, was different. Sometime after the event he confided to a close friend the story that has since been told and retold.

The posse members were very upset because of the stabbing death of their young friend and when they discovered the hat with a colorful band and a gold coin on the table in the cabin, any doubt as to Charles' being the robber was erased.

Having decided his guilt, they retrieved a rope from one of the horses and a wooden crate from the shack and put Charles in the hanging position. Cutter did ask if Charles wanted to say anything, to which he sneered "You'll never find it." Cutter kicked the box from under Charles' feet and the men left, with Charles swinging from a Cypress tree and his dog wolves lying dead at his feet.

Several weeks later, Cutter and the storyteller, whose name was Levi, decided to go back and try to find the gold and cash, convinced Charles had probably buried it.

As Levi told it, they marked likely possibilities based on trees, vegetation, stumps, and so on and then started digging.

When they had reached a depth of perhaps one foot, they heard a low sound that didn't blend in with the normal sounds of the swamp. They stopped digging, listened briefly, but didn't hear the sound, so they began digging again. The noise started again, louder, and it was obviously a growl from some beast. Again, they stopped and looked around. No noise, no creature.

They started digging again and this time the growling became ferocious and so loud, it overwhelmed them.

Close to panic, Cutter and Levi took a quick look at each other, decided it was getting late, and promptly left.

A few days later, Cutter convinced Levi to give it another go, reminding him there was a lot of money and gold somewhere around the shack.

This time, as they were about to dig, there was a creaking sound. They looked around and saw that what was left of Charles was swinging gently from his rope. Attributing this to the wind, they began digging. The growling started and became louder and more ferocious the deeper they dug. They dug faster, then the shovel hit something solid, but before they could react, something grabbed and pulled at the digging end of the shovel, accompanied by the most frightening snarl either man had ever heard.

Levi fell backwards in his haste to drop the shovel and moved away from the hole. Cutter grabbed his shotgun and hurried to Levi's aid just as a barely visible apparition materialized behind the hole. Cutter fired both barrels of his shotgun at the figure with no effect. It felt as though they could feel the hot breath of whatever was snarling. The apparition moved toward them, but by now Levi was on his feet and they were both running for the horses.

They left and never returned, but when the story regarding the true location and circumstances of Charles' death came out, others did. The lure of treasure is compelling.

There were subsequent stories about treasure hunters being spooked by the ferocious dog wolves and Charles. In at least one case, a fellow came out of the swamp with a nasty bite on his arm which he attributed to a ferocious beast he couldn't see.

No one ever found the treasure, or if they did it was not reported.

There are descendants of the men who first dug who think they know generally the location of Indian Charles' shack. They state they have never been there but would be happy to tell you where to go.

Chapter 7

Bartram Trail Incident

One Saturday evening a few miles west of town on a part of Bartram Trail that runs along the Saint Johns River, a local known to all, Joe, showed up at the only watering hole in the area. In the 1930's, there weren't many people along that part of the river, so the one and only drinking establishment was popular, particularly on Saturdays. As the story goes, patrons were dumbfounded when Joe, visibly shaken and very pale exclaimed that he had just seen a bunch of ghosts! Now Joe was a fellow who worked hard but also enjoyed his drinking, though all agreed he did not seem drunk. The patrons tried to calm Joe and asked him what had happened.

It seems that Joe was driving his old, beat up roadster down the road when he saw something in the swampy area between the road and the river. This was a time when people looked out for each other, owing to the sparse population, so Joe pulled over and walked back down the road to see if anyone needed help. He didn't have a light, but there was a partial moon with some clouds, and the moon's reflection off the river allowed him to see into the swampy area.

As he approached, he could hear voices, more than two he thought, but could not see any movement. He called out and the voices stopped. He moved further into the area, stopped and listened. Suddenly, the wind died, and he could just make out the blurry forms of three or four people, or what he surmised had to be people. Their forms were wavy, not clearly defined.

The voices started again, as if in conversation, speaking in what he referred to as a "funny way". He moved closer and called out. The voices stopped, the forms seemed to glow, and disappeared. Joe ran to his car and left, arriving at the tavern shortly after, visibly shaken.

A couple of the men volunteered to go back with Joe to see what they could find. He reluctantly agreed. They returned to the area and looked around, called out and seeing or hearing nothing, returned to the tavern.

Joe was so emphatic about what he had seen and heard; the men found it hard not to believe him. They all had heard stories about "strange occurrences" along this part of the river road, named in honor of the famous naturalist, William Bartram.

Well known in these parts, the well documented story is referred to as the Bartram Trail Incident.

Around 1840, a stagecoach was transporting a Shakespearean acting group from Saint

Augustine to another destination. In the very vicinity were Joe had his experience, the group was ambushed by several Indians, possibly Seminoles, and five of the actors were killed.

The indians showed up in town several hours later wearing the actors' costumes. It wasn't long before local authorities put two and two together, and the indians were hung.

There were a few reports before Joe's sighting, usually at night by fishermen trolling the edge of the swamps who said they had heard or witnessed scenes like what Joe described.

One such accounting was told by two alligator hunters. They had arrived by boat at the same part of the river well before sunrise, a good time to spot and catch young gators. Their method was not for the faint of heart because it involved one hunter entering the water, about waist deep, with an eight-foot coiled cord clamped between his teeth, leaving his hands free. The other hunter's job was to keep a light on the gator while the catcher got the gator's head in a choke hold with one arm, quickly grabbing the coil of rope with the other and wrapping the gator's snout so he couldn't bite. They would then load the gator in the boat, but on this morning, they had trouble getting the gator in, so the boatman entered the water, pulled the boat into the swamp and helped his partner wrestle the beast into the craft.

The two men stood in ankle deep swamp trying to catch their breath when it occurred to them that there were no early morning river sounds; no crickets or other insects, birds, squirrels and so on. This could sometimes mean a predator was about, so they began scanning the area.

As they turned toward the road, several feet into the swamp where it was dry, there stood several people or what appeared to be people, staring back at them. Just at that moment, the sun began rising to the rear of the figures, silhouetting their dim forms. They seemed to bow to the two hunters, and then slowly disappeared.

In the 1940's a group of teenagers familiar with the stories decided to see for themselves. Since it is very dark along the river, they chose a moonlit night to aid their vision. It was obvious that none expected to see anything, but it was a good way to kill time. Their timing was apparently good because they returned to town several hours later, very scared and reported to the sheriff's office that they had seen and heard ghosts. One of the girls said that the voices sounded English and they were speaking as if in a play. She had read Shakespeare in school and insisted that was what she heard. The sheriff's deputy was not amused, but he took two of the kids back to the scene. The others wouldn't go. The deputy's incident report stated that he didn't see anything, but he did hear briefly what could be described as clapping.

The deputy, having been raised in the area, and familiar with some of the stories, also stated that he didn't believe the kids were pulling a prank and in fact believed what they said. No disciplinary action was taken.

Chapter 8

Matanzas

Bill's job change brought him from Indiana to St. Augustine, Florida. He quickly discovered the Atlantic Ocean and inlets offered many forms of recreation unlike those found in his land locked Indiana. Bill developed a passion for fishing the area and was particularly fond of surf fishing and fishing the many bridges. He was delighted when he met another recent transplant, Ted, who shared his enthusiasm. When Ted suggested they check out the Matanzas Inlet area, Bill eagerly agreed. They had both heard that surf fishing around the south point of the inlet at night could be productive.

The two young men chose a moonlit night with calm winds promised by the local forecaster. It was mid-September, and the air was just right; not too hot or cold.

They parked their truck just off the road, grabbed fishing tackle and headed to the oceanside, planning to fish the beach around the point into the inlet.

The first spot they chose offered little action, so they decided to move further in. They had just walked under the bridge headed around the point when Bill stopped, shushed Ted and began scanning the dunes and listening. Finally, Ted asked what he was doing. Bill said he heard a noise like metal clanking from the direction of the dunes. Ted pointed out that they had not seen a single soul since they arrived, so it was most likely the slight wind, or something washed up by the ocean.

They started walking again, and within seconds they both heard noises. They agreed it did indeed sound like metal clanking, as if someone was walking with loose metal objects striking each other. They decided to leave their fishing gear in place and head up the dunes to investigate.

The noise could be heard intermittently as they neared the top of the dunes. They stopped when what sounded like the murmurs of several people could be heard, along with the clanking. Educated men, not easily frightened, they proceeded to the top of the dunes, expecting to find campers or similar activities.

Instead, what they found left them frozen in place!

Aided by the light of the moon, interrupted only slightly by a few passing clouds, they could make out, just barely, several figures moving about. The figures, while human, appeared shadowy, as if not totally formed. There were dozens, some fading in and out of sight, and some that did not have heads!

The mumbling or whispering sounds continued, with the slight, almost aimless movement of the shadowy figures. The two men would report later that whatever was being spoken was not English, but some foreign tongue.

After a few moments, the murmurings quieted, and the figures stopped their slow aimless movement. Things became very quiet. The men said it was as if the strange group had discovered their presence and was staring at them, though they confessed they could not see eyes, or in fact some heads but rather that it just felt that way. The fishermen and shadowy figures observed each other for several minutes.

Then, very slowly, in ones and twos, the figures began fading away until nothing could be seen or heard but the wind, palmettos rustling and the small waves of the shimmering inlet. Not sure what they had experienced, but also not panicked, Bill and Ted decided to retrieve their gear and head back towards the bridge.

As they approached the small two-lane road that went over the bridge, another vehicle pulled onto the shoulder. The occupant gathered something from the truck bed, then headed for the bridge. They could now see his rods outlined in the moonlight, so deducted he was doing a little bridge fishing. They decided that was a good idea and headed up the bank to the bridge.

The friendly old-timer welcomed the company, and the men began to fish. The old man had been in the area all his life and enjoyed talking so it wasn't long before they knew a lot about each other. Bill decided to casually mention what he and Ted had experienced. The old man grunted, chuckled, and told them that what they probably saw was all those Frenchmen the Spanish butchered back in the old days. The old gentleman's explanation was obviously based on stories that had been passed down by locals for many years, but it was enough to cause both men to agree to research the tales.

Their research revealed that in 1565 Menendez, the founder of Saint Augustine was establishing Spanish positions in the area. He was aware that there was a fleet of French ships hovering off both Florida and Georgia coasts but marched first on the French at Ft Caroline north of St Augustine. Menendez captured Fort Caroline and slew the entire garrison except women, children and youths not under arms.

Now Menendez turned his attention to the French ships, which in the aftermath of a violent hurricane, were wrecked and scattered along the coast all the way south to present Cape Canaveral. Most of the French sailors perished, but some made it to shore and headed north toward Saint Augustine.

Upon his return to Saint Augustine after capturing Fort Caroline, Menendez learned that a large group of the wrecked sailors had been spotted near the Matanzas Inlet. He led a small group of soldiers to the area where he found over a hundred desperate sailors who quickly surrendered. Greatly outnumbered by the weary, probably unarmed sailors and having nowhere to house prisoners, Menendez marched them in small groups over the sand dunes where he offered them a choice; convert to Catholicism or die. As devout Protestants, all but a handful of the Frenchman refused and were immediately put to the sword. This almost certainly included some beheadings. The survivors were subsequently used as slave labor.

Several days later, another group of the shipwrecked sailors showed up, and they too were promptly dispatched. Included in this group was the leader of the French expedition, Jean Ribault.

For years, stories surrounding these historical events have thrived, along with the occasional reports of strange encounters such as Bill and Ted experienced.

In one such incident, a couple returning from Flagler beach to Saint Augustine one late night reported an unusual sighting.

As the couple crossed the bridge northbound over the inlet, what appeared to be a bedraggled group of men was suddenly in the car's headlights. The headlights seemed to pass through the figures. The driver braked and the car also passed through the figures, literally. Nothing hit or damaged the car, though it did hit the road's steep shoulder when the driver swerved. Upon exiting the car, nothing unusual could be seen.

A group of teenagers some years later, while sitting around a bonfire on the top of the dunes, kept getting the feeling that something was around them, and some could hear low murmurs. Understandably they relocated their party to the beach side of the dunes.

Finally, it was reported more than one time that while driving A1A in that area during ground fog conditions, an interesting phenomenon occurred. As drivers slowed because of low visibility, the fog seemed to form into shapes, described as the misty, swirling likeness of ghostly figures. Drivers who stopped their vehicles suggested the apparitions would waiver briefly, then float towards the sand dunes. There were no reports, however, of anyone following them.

Bill and Ted decided, out of respect, to confine their future night fishing to the bridge.

Chapter Nine

The Portrait

About 18 miles west of Saint Augustine, just outside the small farm town of Hastings, is a 2000-acre farm. Though the main house sits well back from the major road connecting Hastings and Palatka, it can easily be seen, situated among large beautiful trees.

Locals, however, are wary of the farmhouse at night. They claim that for many years, when passing by the house, one can see lights going on and off upstairs and on occasion, a figure standing in one of the upstairs windows. The problem: this occurred off and on during periods when the house was not occupied, and often was not connected to electricity.

The house was built by a wealthy relative of Henry Flagler in the late 1800s to pursue a farming venture. He did that, growing vegetables for Saint Augustine and the surrounding area. After a few years, because of ill health, he moved to Saint Augustine. By then, there were many more residents of Hastings, including farmers. The little town thrived producing vegetables, including several potato farms, which led to Hastings' designation as the "potato capitol of Florida".

Though the town remained small, it did become a railroad stop around 1900 and was home to several wealthy farmers. Reportedly, the quiet little town was a favorite stopping place for Al Capone and his fellow mobsters during their trips from the North to Miami. They would sometimes stay for a few days in an old two-story hotel located across from the train station. Thoughts were that because there were only two ways in and out of town, they could stroll and relax without worrying about aggressive action by their competitors or the local law. A sanctuary of sorts.

The farm and house changed owners two or three times and somewhere between the late 1930s and mid-1940s, a wealthy local bought it for his son William. William was interested in trying his hand at running a farm. He was a good-looking lad, popular with the ladies, reputed to have broken more than one heart. But he was also industrious.

He set about managing the farm, and since cooking was not one of his interests or skills, he hired a young housekeeper who took up residence in the house and managed the household duties.

Jane was described as plain, though not ugly and could be quick tempered. She was very happy with the arrangement because, for quite some time, she had admired William from afar. Given her plain appearance, her admiration had never been returned by the young lad. Nevertheless, as time passed, she became obsessed with him, and as sometimes happens when a young couple lives in proximity, they began an affair.

Jane was in a state of bliss, and when William, a novice painter, asked if he could paint her portrait, she took this as a sign of affection, which was apparently not the case. The portrait was mediocre at best. Her image was described as having "freaky" eyes, but she was delighted. Over the objection of William, she insisted on hanging it over the living room fireplace.

As William began to get his farming operation running smoothly, he became part of the local social scene again. Since this did not include Jane, she became distressed that her lover was slighting her. When news of his sexual exploits reached her, she reacted most aggressively, confronting him upon his return one evening. She reiterated her love for him, which he stated was misplaced because he had no love for her. Broken hearted, she flew into a furious rage, grabbed a knife and stabbed him repeatedly as he turned to go down the stairs. Realizing what she had done, she then killed herself.

The house sat empty for several years, during which farmworkers reported noises, including sobbing sounds and wails coming from the house. They would go no closer to the house than required while working. Finally, the house was sold to a couple from New York. Oblivious to what had occurred, they rented a place in town temporarily so they could work on the house.

As the unsuspecting owners started their work, they would sometimes hear strange sounds and would find the upstairs lights on when neither of them had been up there. They attributed this to the age of the house and perhaps varmints. Those thoughts changed soon after.

The new owners arrived at the house one morning with the goal of prepping the downstairs walls for painting. They set about moving furniture away from the walls. There were several pictures, paintings, and other doodads hanging on the walls; including Jane's portrait over the fireplace mantle.

As they removed the wall ornaments and pulled a variety of nails and hooks from the walls, they had a sensation of being watched. They heard a series of distinct squeaking sounds as if someone was coming down the stairs on old, creaky boards. It had begun raining so they attributed this to a combination of old wood and wind.

The man set a step stool in front of the fireplace to remove the portrait. As he reached for the painting, which they had both agreed was hideous, he heard his wife gasp. He turned his head toward her and saw that she was staring at the staircase. There, on the bottom landing was an apparition, moving like heat rising from a hot road, with air moving like ribbons bouncing on strings in a random fashion. He unconsciously lifted the painting from its hook and stepped off the stool, but as he did so, a chair flew across the room, narrowly missing his wife. The temperature dropped and they could see their breath coming in rapid bursts of fright. They shivered from the frigid air that filled the room.

He dropped the painting as the apparition grew slightly brighter and seemed to take form; perhaps a woman. He opened his mouth to instruct his wife to move toward the door, but instead, started gagging, as she did. They put their hands over their mouths as a foul stench filled their nostrils. As they bolted for the door, a table crashed against the wall and they heard what was described as a shriek, followed by sobbing behind them. They ran into the yard, and the door slammed shut violently behind them.

The couple left town, and within weeks the house was listed for sale. Unfortunately, the couple had told what they experienced to the hardware store owner, from whom they had made several purchases for the house renovation. His comment was that though there had been sightings of a figure in the window and lights going on and off, he had never heard of anything else. This only verified to the couple that they had made the right decision to sell.

Of course, the small-town hardware store was the hub of town business, so it wasn't long before everyone knew the strange story. Because of this no doubt, the house again sat empty for a long time.

Finally, the house was bought by a relative newcomer. He also bought two other farms nearby. His plan with this house, unaware of its complete history, was to use it as offices to run all three farms. He was familiar with some of the house's history, but not about the previous owner's experience. He had heard the stories about lights going on and off but was not alarmed, attributing that story as the reason he had gotten a great deal on the old house.

Soon after, the new owner arrived at the house with two contractors to plan the downstairs office renovations. As they entered, they had an experience like the previous owners. He contacted them to learn what they knew. He asked them to describe in detail what happened, and they did. He restated back to them what they had told him including, the removal of Jane's portrait, which seemed to precipitate events. They verified he had their recounting correct. The businessman, now stuck with this situation, decided it was time to make a deal.

The next day he arrived at the house with a single purpose. He opened the door and entered, frigid air and a horrible stench met him. He held his breath and headed for the step stool and painting. As he got to the stool and reached for the painting, he became aware of movement behind him and the sound of sobbing. He grabbed the portrait, mounted the stool, and hung it back in place. Almost immediately the air became normal, and the sobbing stopped.

He stepped outside and called the contractors, assuring them everything was normal, and they could begin work. Things were more normal, but not completely.

Offices were installed downstairs, but the upstairs plans were changed. The farm staff kept reporting that when they went up there, they felt like they were being watched, and many times while downstairs working, they could hear footsteps and sobbing upstairs, when no one was up there.

The owner finally closed off the upstairs, reiterated previous instructions to never touch Jane's portrait, and things once again returned to normal -- except for the occasional passerby reports of lights upstairs going on and off and a figure in the window.

Chapter Ten

Pirates on the River

Saint Augustine tale tellers can regale one with the exploits of pirates raiding the Old Town, all well documented events. Less known and less documented are the forays of one pirate band into the Saint Johns River, a few miles west of town.

Several years ago, a visiting bass fisherman headed his boat into a fair size slew at the mouth of Six Mile Creek. Being unfamiliar with the area, he was not aware of what all locals knew about the slew. In the first place there are no fish to be caught there. No one knows why, because that entire area of the river is plentiful with fish. But not in this slew. Then there is the line hanging problem. Something large is on the bottom and a fishhook will find it pronto! Lastly, people have reported 'things' in this slew.

The fisherman stopped his boat and lowered his line into the water. Were he more knowledgeable, he would have noticed that it was very quiet on the slew. No insect, bird, or other creature noises which one can always hear on the river near banks. A hot breeze started blowing over him. The slew is well off the river, surrounded by giant trees and swamps. Its mouth is oriented such that a breeze can't find its way in.

Suddenly, the water around his boat started bubbling. What appeared to be smoke rose up out of the bubbles. He could faintly hear what he described as chanting and the clinks of metal on metal. His line went taunt. He jerked the rod, discovering he was clearly hung. He pulled on the line, the rod tip bending double, but not bouncing, as a fish would cause. Something started pulling the line down. He held firmly to the rod until the line snapped, throwing him backwards into a heap on the boat bottom. The voices grew louder, and he could hear crackly sounds, like the sound of burning wood. He quickly departed.

The story told to explain these events is intriguing. In the very early 1800s, the Saint Johns River area was only sparsely inhabited. Indians had a large camp somewhere between the Six Mile Creek area and Black Creek, a few miles north on the river. Both creeks are wide and very deep. The indians hunted and fished the area and foraged all the way up into Georgia and occasionally went as far as the ocean, where the St John's empties. There was an uneasy alliance between the indians and the few settlers. They traded and tolerated each other.

One day, a small pirate ship sailed from the ocean into the river. Where they came from, or why they were in the river, was a mystery to both the indians and settlers. The pirates created an encampment down one of the large creeks, well out of the main river. It was reported to be near the indian camp.

Soon, the ship was seen leaving the river ocean bound. A small contingent was left to man their camp. A few weeks later, this ship returned, and they soon began trading with both the indians and settlers. After a few weeks the ship would leave again. It became evident the pirates were preying on merchant ships in the Atlantic and returning to the river to rest and trade.

This unusual situation seemed to work well for all parties concerned because the pirates' stolen bounty provided merchandise and supplies otherwise hard to come by for both indians and settlers. This unspoken mutual arrangement soon changed.

It is reported that the pirates took an interest in some of the indian women during trading events. This behavior did not set well with the protective warriors.

During one such event where pillaged rum flowed freely, the pirates apparently took too many liberties, and the indians slaughtered the lot. They took what they wanted, burned the few buildings and left.

The settlers found themselves with a dilemma. What to do? They could not go after the guilty parties because they were far outnumbered; they could not win a war with the indians.

The decision was made to load the pirate bodies onto the ship, still moored at the camp, and sail it further into the river where it would be burned and sunk. They chose the large slew at the mouth of Six Mile Creek. The task was accomplished, and things apparently returned to normal.

In recent decades the Outback Crab Shack Restaurant and Bar, about one mile into the Six Mile Creek, was built and became very popular with boaters who would come in by water, both day and night. The restaurant staff began getting inquiries from boaters regarding the slew area. This included questions about a fire burning in this slew. Were there camp areas there? Absolutely not! It's all swamp and marsh. Then what is the source of the fire? Other unexplained reports included multiple sightings of a ragged flag flying from a pole in the same area.

One group of yachters stopped to check their own craft for fire because of a strong smoke smell in that area. They also reported noise which they described as a free for all, much like men fighting.

Local legend has it that the scallywag pirates probably received their just reward, but their restless spirits still hang around their sunken ship. One thing is for certain; they are not good for fishing!

Chapter Eleven

Tolomato

    Tolomato Cemetery is located on Cordova Street just south of Orange Street and is named after a Tolomato Indian village that was located, in part, on this site. After the Seven Year War in Europe was lost by Spain, England became the new owner of Florida. The Spanish, along with the few remaining Timucuan Indians, fled to Cuba. At that time, Tolomato became a Catholic Cemetery. It dates to the early 1700's and was used as a cemetery until 1884. A variety of ethnic groups are buried there, including people from Spain, Cuba, Ireland, Minorca, Italy, Greece, Africa, Haiti, France and America. It also includes both union and confederate soldiers from the civil war.

    The small mausoleum located at the rear of the cemetery was said to have contained a bishop whose body exploded during his viewing at the cathedral. His body pieces were gathered up and brought to the mausoleum and subsequently sent to Cuba. One of the many stories about Tolomato's hauntings is the bishop being seen on occasion searching for his missing wooden teeth. There is also the occasional sighting of a young boy perched in one of the large oak trees. Another involves a report by out of towners.

In the 1970s, a middle age tourist couple was taking a late evening stroll down the sidewalk which fronts the cemetery. The cemetery, fenced and locked, is generally not open to the public. There is, however, an indentation in the short mortar wall where one may step over to read the history displayed on a brass plate. The vantage point also offers an unobstructed view of several grave markers.

The couple diverted from the sidewalk to read the placard.

The woman asked her husband to take a picture of her by the placard, and as he backed toward the street to get a wider shot, his wife suddenly bent backwards as if being grabbed from behind by her shoulders. She yelled that something was pulling her and was then suddenly thrust forward into her husband, knocking them both to the ground. At the same time, they were both pelted with leaves and twigs as if a giant blower had scattered the ground debris from the cemetery. They struggled to their feet as an even stronger gust of air blew more debris all over them. There were several small, pale lights slightly above the ground in the cemetery, accompanied by a foul smell so overwhelming the woman gagged.

The light began transforming into something which they described as a hollow form, and as it grew larger, a low snarling sound could be heard.

The wind suddenly stopped in a final hot rush of air as the lights and sound dissipated into the night.

Some years later, an event occurred in almost the exact spot of the tourist experience. That story, and others, were shared with me by Hattie.

Hattie was an elderly black woman; how old was anybody's guess, but she was a descendant of the first freed slaves who settled and established the Lincolnville section of Saint Augustine. She still lived in one of the old small family houses.

Hattie was a delight. She was a small, withered, old lady. Snow white hair highlighted a face so wrinkled that her features were difficult to distinguish. Despite this, her sinewy appearing body, remarkable energy and enthusiasm made her seem youthful.

Her favorite pastime was riding the streets of Saint Augustine on her three-wheel bicycle, waving and saying hello to all passerby's; and telling stories.

I enjoyed many of her stories, but one is particularly memorable because of her demeanor and emotion in the telling. She was reliving it, and it scared her.

Hattie had ridden her bike past Tolomato thousands of times and even said she saw the young boy in the tree in the cemetery more than one time. It didn't bother her. Said it was just a spirit trying to find its way home. One evening, she experienced something that did get her attention, and could even be viewed as supporting evidence of the tourists' report in its similarity.

As she approached the cemetery, she became conscious that she was thinking about scenes that were unfamiliar to her. She seemed to be recalling scenes from another person's memory; a tall ship, it's majestic sails full in the wind sliding past the old fort, soldiers on horses galloping through the streets and people running.

Adjacent to the cemetery, Hatti glimpsed a faint glow towards the rear of the graveyard. She knew it was not a light because it moved toward her, growing larger as its shape transformed.

The form continued toward her; its' shape more defined; perhaps a young boy? She began to dismount from her bike so she could move to the fence. Her intent was to communicate with the apparition, but she could not move. Something was holding her. Struggle as she might, she could not get off the bike.

The form was now stationary, no longer moving toward her.

It began drifting further away as debris from the cemetery pelted her. Her bike started shaking, the loose fenders making a loud clattering sound as they banged against the frame.

Hattie's hat flew off and a noise in the swirling leaves popped and cracked. An image of a small electrical arc outlined the shape of something unrecognizable, much larger than the other form which had now retreated to the rear of the cemetery.

Hattie struggled to free her hands from the bike's handlebars but couldn't. The bike rose off the ground, the wheels spinning wildly, fenders clanging. The light impulses danced around her ferociously, now accompanied by a deep, hoarse moaning sound.

As quickly as it had begun, the noise and light show stopped, and the bike crashed to the ground, spilling the now freed Hattie. The light at the rear of the graveyard was gone and the only movement was a small whirlwind of debris moving across the ground, then dropping onto one of the graves.

Hattie's explanation was that the first light was a young spirit trying to get to the other side and the larger more violent form was keeping it in and didn't want Hattie interfering.

Another good friend of mine, Dan, discovered from Tolomato that sometimes pranks can backfire.

Dan was born in the early 1940s and grew up one block from the rear of the cemetery, just off Orange Street.

One summer when Dan was about 12 years old, he befriended a couple of boys one or two years younger than he. They were visiting one of Dan's neighbors for a few days.

In the boredom of summer, and the boys being boys, Dan decided to enlist his two friends, Riley and Matt, to play a joke on the visiting youngsters. The plan was to take them into the cemetery at night and scare them. Riley was to hide behind a tree where they would hang a sheet with two eye holes. At Dan's signal, Riley would raise the sheet and shine a light up through it to give the appearance of a dancing apparition. At the same time, Matt, who would be hiding a few feet from Riley, would moan and release his mother's cat, whom they had surreptitiously borrowed.

Dan reports the prank came off without a hitch. The signal was given, the lighted ghost sprang up, there was a moan, and the cat battled through the vegetation right at Dan and his guests.

The two young boys ran to the fence, climbed and fell over it and were gone. Dan and company began laughing and regaling their joke.

That is, until something else caught their attention. They could hear a distinct noise toward the center of the cemetery. As they peered through the darkness toward the sound, a faint glow accompanied by swirling leaves seemed to rise from one of the graves.

They too climbed and fell over the fence. Dan swears this happened. But that was not the end of it.

Just a few days later, Dan was performing his duties at the oldest drug store, located next to Tolomato. His summer job was to show up just before closing, sweep and mop and take all the trash to the dumpsters located at the rear of the store, about 15 feet from the cemetery.

It was dark by the time he finished inside and headed through the now empty parking lot with his first bags of trash. A dog sniffing around the dumpster was the only thing moving.

As Dan neared the dumping area, a light caught his eye in the cemetery. He turned and saw what looked like bunched up electrical sparks moving toward him across the cemetery.

The dog had his hackles up, his lips curled back from his teeth as his growl grew louder. Suddenly, his courage deserted him and with a frightened yelp, he scuttled away, tail tucked between his legs.

Dan's first thought was that his friends were having more fun at his expense. The dancing flashes grew larger and a shape resembling a human form could be seen. A loud, indescribable cry came from the now mass of swirling, arcing sparks. A large, deep hollowness could be seen where eyes should have been.

The security light over the dumpster exploded in a maze of sparks as trees in the cemetery started rattling and whipping around furiously. A foul smell became evident as the shape grew even larger.

Dan turned and ran to the safety of the drugstore where Ray was coming out with the rest of the trash. Ray walked past, somewhat agitated that he was doing Dan's job. He continued to the dumpster where he deposited the bags, including the two, Dan had dropped when he ran. The cemetery was perfectly quiet and still.

To this day, Dan will not go close to the cemetery at night by himself.

Chapter Twelve
The Feather

John and Mary were a young thirtyish couple, educated and each successful professionally in their own right. They had relocated to Saint Augustine from the Midwest a couple of years ago. Both had grown up in a rural ranch environment and shared a passion for the outdoors. Though they loved Saint Augustine and the many social activities and events, they frequently had the urge to rough it.

.   John had discovered a large area on the west side of the Saint Johns River a few miles west of town and suggested a boating and camping excursion. Mary enthusiastically agreed.

The JP Hall Wilderness, as the name implies, is several thousand acres of swamps and wilderness lands donated to the state many years ago. It's located in the area starting west of the Shands Bridge and occupies the entire area east to the river and south from the bridge for several miles. Only wild creatures live there because of its protected status. There is a rough trail the adventurous can use, but as signs will tell you, leave the trail at your own peril. It is heavily wooded with centuries old growth, thick brush and becomes very swampy toward the river. Snakes abound.

John wanted to camp on the river and could readily see that getting to the riverbank from the roadside in the wilderness was not a good idea. It was decided to go by boat after a friend showed him an area on the map that one, if careful, could reach by boat.

On a coldish, early November morning, they launched the boat at Trout Creek Marina and headed downriver. John had no trouble finding the area but could see he would need to be very careful getting in. The shoreline was thick with reeds, and limbs could be seen sticking up from the water. When his depth gauge reached four feet, he raised the outboard motor and began poling the boat to the shore. He headed for a spot that sloped upward from the river knowing it should be less swampy and more dry.

The bow of the boat hit bottom, so he began climbing out to pull it the remainder of the way to shore. He was halfway out when Mary yelled, "Look out!" A large shrieking bird was dive bombing them, as if to drive them away. John grabbed the bow rope and pulled the craft and Mary to shore, all the while ducking the dives of the bird. He secured the bow rope to a tree just as the bird ceased his attack and flew out over the river. A quick look around suggested they had chosen a good location, so they began erecting the tent. Having done that, Mary started laying out sleeping bags and setting up their small camp table while John collected wood for a fire. A few feet from their site, he noticed the remains of a campfire, obviously used quite some time ago, but clearly charcoaled wood remains from a fire. He was surprised, given the remote location.

John got a small fire going and suggested they walk down to the river edge to see if the area was clear enough to fish without getting hung. John noticed an open area about eight feet across surrounded by reeds and lily pads, but fishable. Several minutes later, with four fish in hand, darkness had fallen, and they decided to cook their catch.

Picking their way up the rough slope, John could see their fading fire. Then he saw movement. There was something by the fire, like a lump. Exercising more caution, he touched Mary and pointed toward the fire. They moved slowly and quietly forward, not sure if they were seeing something dangerous or harmless.

The pair could now see that something or someone was putting wood on the fire. As soon as John could tell it was a human, he called out. The figure, now only a few feet away, rose from a squatting position and turned toward them. In the dim flickering glow from the fire they could see the stranger was dressed in what appeared to be leather breaches and was shirtless, odd because of the cool weather.

John spoke to the man again, but without answering, he moved past them down the slope. As he passed, they could see he had a leather band around his head. He passed silently; not even leaves or twigs could be heard crunching under his footsteps. He walked into the river, disappearing, or rather fading away, before he was even knee deep. As he faded, a large bird like the one they encountered earlier swooped out of the dark sky and perched on his up raised arm.

There was an animated discussion regarding their next course of action. Sleep seemed out of the question given what they had experienced, so it was decided to head back to the fish camp, leave the boat moored overnight and return for their gear the next day.

They arrived at Trout Creek Marina to find Joe closing shop and surprised at their presence since they had arranged to leave their car overnight. Under Joe's questioning look, they explained they had indeed set up camp and would need to return for their gear the next day. Now very curious, Joe asked where their camp was located. When they told him, he responded that it was somewhat of a rough area to camp. In the silence that followed, he asked if they had seen something.

Mary finally acknowledged that though it sounded foolish, they were sure they had seen a man in their camp who just faded away. Joe asked what kind of man. Mary answered that he appeared to be dressed like an indian, except that he had a beard and she always thought indian's didn't have beards. John agreed with her description. Joe replied that there was a story about that area told through the years about a fellow named Matthew Cordova. John and Mary implored him to tell them.

In the late fifteen hundreds, the newly arrived Spanish would occasionally send out small groups of soldiers from the fort to survey the surrounding areas. For the soldiers, it was not a mission to volunteer for. It rained in the swamps all the time, or so it seemed. The smoldering heat and mosquitoes were just as bad. One such group had been out several weeks when they stumbled onto a small indian village, and after some tense moments, determined the indians to be friendly, though aloof. The captain ordered camp to be set up adjacent to the village to allow the party to rest and regroup before continuing on with the surveying mission.

The indians, while not thrilled the soldiers were there, seemed to tolerate their presence, though largely choosing to ignore them. The captain told his men to be friendly but cautious.

A very young Matthew Cordova was likely the youngest member of this party. While the other soldiers found the indians uninteresting, Cordova was awed. The contrast between the dress of the soldiers, in their heavy clothes and armor, and the savages in loincloth, the women topless, was remarkable. They were very dark and did not seem to be bothered by the oppressive heat and constant bugs. Their days seemed to be spent hunting for food, fishing and repairing their strange little boats. Occasionally, they played games with much laughter and animated movements. Most of the soldiers were suspicious or afraid of the savages. But Cordova found them fascinating and took every opportunity to learn their ways and communicate with them, though he made little progress in either area.

The indians were very clannish and took offense to any attention an outsider might show their women. The women, however, were more curious about the strange looking intruders.

Cordova's interaction with the indians did not go unnoticed by his captain. The day they were preparing to leave camp, he summoned Matthew and directed him to stay with the indians for a few months. His job would be to learn as much as he could about their ways, then make his way back to the fort with his report. It was felt that this information might be useful in future dealings with the tribes. Though surprised, Matthew was elated over this turn of events.

Over the next several weeks, a routine slowly evolved between Matthew and the indians, uneasy at first but eventually transitioning to a more comfortable situation. While the males usually disappeared at sunrise on hunting and fishing parties, sometimes for days, the others stayed close to the village performing various chores. Some males stayed in the village, apparently for protection, and, he suspected, to watch him. Matthew concentrated on learning their ways without being too intrusive.

He soon began participating with the younger boys as they practiced their hunting skills, throwing crudely fashioned spears and shooting arrows at whatever targets attracted their attention. Their enjoyment in showing off and teaching Matthew seemed to please the adults, who grew more comfortable with this strange young man with each passing day.

The indians thought it very strange when Matthew found a young hawk with an injured wing and fashioned a small cage to care for it. As the hawk slowly healed and grew, it took to perching on Matthew's shoulder, something the indians had never witnessed before. A young woman, about Matthew's age, began showing up at Matthew's tent with food for the hawk. Soon they were together most of the time. This did not particularly please the chief, though he did like Matthew.

The hawk finally flew, but after several circles and acrobatics, returned to Matthew's shoulder. This truly impressed the indians. The hawk would disappear for hours, probably hunting, but always returned to Matthew.

Matthew and the young girl became an

item and seemed to be constantly together. Some approved, some didn't. One day they were foraging for berries and roots. The chief's young son, about 12, was with them, as was the hawk. As they poked around the ground for roots, the hawk left Matthew's shoulder and perched on a limb watching them. Suddenly, he swooped down and grabbed a moccasin as it was preparing to strike the boy. Whether the hawk was just catching dinner or trying to save the boy is anybody's guess, but when the event was reported back in the village, Matthew found himself in good favor with the chief.

The chief announced that this stranger had a spiritual link with the wild creatures; proclaimed his totem a feather and accepted him into the tribe. Taking a chance, Matthew asked for the young girl's hand and the chief agreed. Though he had been accepted by the tribe, his marriage very much solidified that fact.

He was still somewhat of a novelty, particularly given the sparse growth of hair on his young face. The tribe's fascination with his hawk and his ability to control it remained. The young boys would clamor to go with him to watch the hawk hunt small rodents and snakes and then always return to Mathew's arm. When other tribal leaders would visit, the chief enjoyed watching their reaction to this strange man who had a pet hawk. They too agreed he had a special gift.

Matthew's days were passed spearing

fish and accompanying the braves on hunting parties. He looked forward to evenings around the campfire. Having picked up enough of their language to understand the gist of most things said, he marveled at their stories and the simple pleasures they shared. He particularly enjoyed swimming with his bride in the river, an almost daily occurrence. They would play and laugh like kids, much to the amusement of the others.

Time was a relative thing in this way of life, and Matthew was not sure how long he had been there; perhaps many months, even a year or more. He began pondering his dilemma. Surely, he would be missed by now. Would the captain send a party to look for him? Should he go back? His bride would never be accepted, even if allowed back at the Fort. Anyway, how would he support her on his paupers pay? He could even be sent away on other excursions for months, or even forever. What would she do?

Though always a loyal young soldier, his love for his bride made his decision easy. He would not return, and if they came in search of him, he would hide, confident the tribe would not reveal his status.

Many more months passed, and no one came. The daily routines continued until one day as he and his bride were swimming in the river, tragedy struck. The girl was playfully splashing water as Matthew was washing an animal hide for tanning in the shallow water. She challenged him to chase her and began swimming further out. Undeterred, he continued his task, glancing out at her occasionally. His hawk, circling the girl, began shrieking. He looked up to see her struggling, as if something was pulling her under. Without hesitation he dropped the hide and began swimming to her. She went under and did not come up. Matthew arrived at the area where he had last seen her and began diving under the water, feeling for her in the dark, brackish water. He could not find her and finally became so exhausted, he too started struggling, but would not head back to shore.

By now several braves had heard the commotion, and seeing Matthew's predicament, two of them swam to his aid and against his will, pulled him to the shore. They held him down until he digested the fact that his bride was gone. He lay on the shore for hours, then slowly went to his tent where he remained for days, refusing food and visits by others. He came out only to walk to the river's edge and gaze out across the vast expanse. The hawk, sensing his emotional distress would perch on a nearby branch, watching him.

This theme played out for weeks until one day near dusk, he walked down to the river, paused at the edge, then slowly started walking out into the water. By the time others on the shore realized what was happening, he was gone.

Soon after, the hawk would frequently start shrieking, which prompted the others to run to the river's edge, where in the distance, the hawk could be seen circling a large swirl in the water. This continued happening and the tribe accepted it as the spirit of Matthew looking for his bride. As time passed, there were even reports that on occasion Matthew could be seen far out diving under the water's surface, searching.

Joe finished his story and waited for the couple's reaction. After a brief silence, John commented that surely Joe was not suggesting that they had seen the ghost of Matthew Cordova. Joe responded that he was just telling a story that had been around a few 100 years, but other people had seen similar things in the past.

The couple drove back to town after assuring Joe they would return for their boat the next day and retrieve their gear from the campsite.

They arrived at the fish camp early the next morning and checked in with Joe. They advised him they were headed back to the camp to get their equipment and should return in a couple of hours. As an afterthought, Mary asked Joe if he recalled where they said the camp was. He sensed her concern, smiled, and stated that as far as he knew, Cordova had never harmed anyone. Blushing at her silliness, Mary thanked him, and they departed.

They found the camp area and John began poling the boat toward the shore, all the while once again being dive bombed by the large hawk. They hit shore and the bird perched on a limb, watching them.

Nothing seemed to be missing, so they set about striking the tent and gathering their gear. They stowed everything but the folding table John had left for last. He approached the table and stopped. He called to Mary who had already gotten in the boat. When she joined him, he asked if she had gotten the filet knife he had left on the table to clean fish. She responded "No" and followed John's stare to the table. There was nothing on it but a long, grayish white feather which turned reddish brown toward the end. They both looked up at the hawk, still watching the activity. Without speaking, John picked up the feather and placed it in a zip lock bag. He folded the table and they left.

When the boat had reached a safe point to lower the motor, John laid the pole down and turned toward the shore. He spoke Mary's name and she followed his gaze. The hazy image of the man they had seen the night before was standing on the shore staring at them. He raised his arm and the hawk swooped down and landed on it. As he turned to head into the woods, another smaller figure could barely be seen joining him. As John and Mary watched, the couple and the hawk slowly disappeared.

They continued staring in silence at the

now empty scene until finally, John cranked the motor and they headed back to the fish camp.

Matthew Cordova and his indian bride are still seen by boaters on occasion, though only briefly. The couple, accompanied by a large bird, seem to appear, then vanish, in an instant.

Chapter 13

Sanksville Cemetery

Stories about haunted cemeteries are plentiful. Cemeteries are a place for the dead; host to the spirits of those departed. For many of us, when we find ourselves among the graves and tombstones, there is a natural inclination to ponder the aftermath of life. Do ghosts reside in some of these graves? Are some trapped somewhere "in between"; or on occasion, do their restless spirits reach out and show themselves?

For those who absolutely scoff at the idea of ghosts, and certainly for skeptics, offer a challenge; go into a deserted graveyard at night, alone, and look around. For those who accept, note their demeanor as they exit the experience. Are they relieved they have finished the challenge? Do they display a tad too much bravado having gotten through it? Of course, if you are a true believer, there is nothing to get through. It's a perfectly normal stroll, no different than a stroll through the park.

My point is that if there are hauntings, then surely a graveyard is a place of all places for that to occur. If the cemetery is remote, off the beaten path, seldom visited, but still has reports of sightings, one might tend to pay more attention. Such is the case regarding Sanksville Cemetery.

This cemetery is several miles west of town, generally boarded by Joe Ashton Rd and County Road 208. Though not in the city limit, the area is considered a part of Saint Augustine.

For ten years, we had an equine riding school across the road from Sanksville Cemetery and can confirm that it is seldom visited. It is not marked on the road, and to get to it, one must use the driveway of a private dwelling located directly in front of it. Those trying to locate the site would not do so unless they had been given specific directions.

While it is difficult to date the cemetery, most agree it is pre civil war. The earliest dated headstone is 1869 though many appear older and are not dated. The Sanks' family owns the cemetery as a result of an ancestor's land purchase many years ago. They also maintain the cemetery.

For several years, despite having few visitors, there have been many sightings in this graveyard. The presence of pale, misty appearing lights over the ground in the graveyard has been seen many times. I was acquainted with the husband and wife who lived in the residence directly in front of the cemetery for three years. They told me that when outside in their back yard at night, they routinely heard what sounded like murmurings and in one instance humming. They also stated that on no occasion did they choose to go into the cemetery to look for the source of these sounds.

The other sightings vary, but two descriptions, reported by several people, three of whom I am personally acquainted with, are very similar.

One involves the appearance in the graveyard of two people; a woman described as very sad looking and a stocky man, both dressed in 19th century attire. Those seeing them state that they appear to be staring back, then slowly fade away. At least, two of these sightings happened during the daylight hours.

The other sighting involves a shadowy group of men, perhaps five or six, who seemed to be wearing soldier uniforms and carrying rifles. It is known that there are civil war soldiers buried here. A couple venturing into the cemetery late at night felt as if they were being watched from the shadows and then began to hear whispers. They started towards the sound and as they neared what appeared to be the source area, the whispers stopped. It became very still and silent. They sensed something and suddenly realized there were shadowy figures all around them and as before, were wearing soldier uniforms. As the couple backtracked towards the entrance, the figures seemed to slowly disappear as they turned and headed to the rear of the cemetery.

On a personal note, on hot humid, summer days, we often taught in the evenings. We had bright lighting for the riding rings, stable, paddock and residence. This lighting dimly illuminated the tree line and gate entrance to Sanksville Cemetery. Lessons ended about 10:00 pm and it took another hour to groom and bed down the horses. Then we'd start securing the farm before retiring for the night.

Countless times, the horses seemed restless without cause and we had the "hair raising on the back of your neck" sensation of being watched. A low, chant like sound could be heard from across the street and misty glowing figures and orbs could be seen in the tree line of Sanksville Cemetery.

Initially, this made us consider moving the school to a new location; but after several weeks of sightings, sensations and sounds without following harmful events; we decided to stay, control our curiosity, and let the entities across the street alone!

Chapter Fourteen

Swamp Girl

Late one evening, a middle-aged couple was traveling south on Highway 13 just west of town. The sky was displaying a three quarters full moon with broken clouds casting shadows intermittently. It had been a perfect night to enjoy the summer concert series on the Plaza in St. Augustine. They were discussing the merits of the performance they had seen.

As the couple approached the small bridge that spans Six Mile Creek, the woman suddenly yelled "watch out," causing the driver to brake hard, just as he saw something run across the road directly in front of them.

After pulling off the road to regain their composure, they agreed that what they had seen was a young girl being chased or followed by a large cat like animal. She had appeared from the Jack Wright Island side of the swamp, crossed the road, and entered the thick swampy area on the other side of the road where she and the animal disappeared. The driver grabbed his flashlight from the glove compartment, climbed down the embankment and aimed the powerful beam toward the swamp as he called out. Nothing could be seen in the thick vegetation and no one answered him back.

He picked his way back up the steep embankment, and over the objections of his frightened wife, walked the remaining few feet to the bridge. Halfway up the bridge he had a more unobstructed view of the creek shoreline as it disappeared into the thick swamp. The beam of his light caught a slight movement, and he thought he heard a low growl. The brush moved again just as an owl's hoot broke the silence, causing him to jump. At his now truly frightened wife's urging, he walked back to the car.

They decided to call the police, feeling that a 12 or 13-year-old girl, as she appeared to be, should not be in a swamp late at night, particularly if she was being chased by a wildcat of some kind. The deputy in that patrol area had been nearby and arrived quickly.

He listened to their story, then politely asked, or stated that perhaps, because of the shadows, they had seen a deer or even a black bear and mistook it for a human. The couple was emphatic that such was not the case. They were certain they had seen a young girl pursued by some creature.

The officer picked his way down the sloping road shoulder and shined his flashlight into the woods as he called out, with no response. He walked back to the couple and told them he would stay around a few more minutes, but the fact was that the sheriffs' office had received similar reports for years in the area around Jack Wright Island. Initially, searches had been conducted, but nothing was ever found. Though unhappy with the deputy's explanation, it was obvious that there was nothing else to be done, so the couple departed.

In an apparent related incident, a boater arrived at Trout Creek Marina just before dusk one evening to report that he had just seen a very young girl in the swamp; in the 'middle of nowhere'. As he moved his boat toward her to see if she needed help, she turned her head as if someone had called her. He got nearer, and she turned and walked toward another person behind her in the distance. That figure was blurry, but it appeared to be Indian; long braided hair and dressed in what appeared to be a leather dress. He was alarmed when a panther appeared out of a palmetto stand and followed the girl. They all disappeared into the thicket.

Folks in this area tell the story of a young girl who lived here with her family during the mid to late 1800's. She was a delightful girl, known for her gentle ways and uncanny ability to relate to animals and other creatures. She befriended a young girl from the indian camp a couple of miles from her home, and together they would nurse injured or ill animals and birds. Their relationship was not condoned by either of the girls' families, so they began meeting in the swamp to play, talk and care for their animals. One day the girl went into the swamp and never returned.

Over the years, the indian girl was seen many times during trading events between her tribe and the settlers. Initially, she was quizzed about the missing girl, but she had no knowledge of her whereabouts. She did say she may have seen her on occasion in the swamp, but she wasn't sure because her friend looked different.

Several years after the girl's disappearance, a trapper reported that while reaching to check one of his traps, a moccasin reared its' head ready to strike. Out of nowhere, a young girl appeared, reached her hand toward the snake and made a shooing motion. The snake slithered away. The trapper turned to thank the girl, but she had joined an older indian woman some distance away. As they headed into the swamp, the young girl slowly disappeared into thin air, along with a panther who had joined her. The older woman could be clearly seen until the foliage enveloped her. He recalled seeing her during trades with the indians.

There were stories over the years that the young girl had a habit of helping people who had ventured into or around the swamp. The horse of one fellow who was hunting ran off, and as he left the swamp after a long walk, he found his horse was tied to a branch at the edge. Another involved a young child who wandered into the swamp while his father was fixing a broken wagon. When he noticed the boy gone, he panicked and ran into the swamp, yelling the child's name. Soon he heard a faint response back toward the road. He ran back and found the child, muddy and scratched, standing by the wagon. The father, in most likely not a gentle manner, asked the boy where he had been. The child related he got lost but the nice girl and her big cat brought him back. The man looked around but saw no other people.

Locals say the young girl did somehow die in the swamp, but her indian friend lived to be very old and could be seen frequently in and around the swamp, many times in the company of a pale apparition of the young girl, in a long gingham dress. These sightings continued for many years along with stories of a helping hand to wayfarers by the young girl in the swamp. Finally, the old indian woman also died.

In modern times, the area has grown quite a bit. The swamp is still there, but no one goes in, so no one gets hurt or lost. Because of this, there are few sightings; except when Swamp Girl ventures out herself.

Chapter Fifteen

The Sea Wall

Should you decide to take a walk along the Saint Augustine seawall, be careful you don't bump into a smartly dressed young army officer and his lady. They have been strolling the wall for almost 200 years.

The sea wall runs along the bayfront of Saint Augustine and provides a wonderful trail for evening walks. It extends from the Castillo de San Marcos going south to the vicinity of Saint Francis Barracks, now home to the headquarters of the Florida National Guard.

The first section of wall was originally built under Spanish ownership and stopped short of the Plaza.

In 1821, the United States took ownership of Saint Augustine, and in 1833 money was allocated to repair the fort, a very important landmark to the locals. The job was given to a young army Lieutenant. The young officer, however, had other plans.

The Lieutenant had met a young lady shortly after he arrived in Saint Augustine and had begun a courtship. His lady lived with her parents directly in front of the bayfront, in one of the large two-story dwellings, built around 1730. The couple often took long evening strolls along the bayfront.

It occurred to the Lieutenant that rather than spending the allocated money for repair to the old fort, it might be more prudent to widen the existing seawall and extend it further south. This was sound reasoning given the violent storms and subsequent erosion along the bayfront. Since that was the case, he decided it should be wide enough to handle the most severe storms and perhaps accommodate a couple walking side by side.

Apparently, he did not seek guidance for his plan from supervisors but chose instead to begin work on the seawall. To appease locals, he made a few minor repairs to the fort.

The young lady's house was perfectly situated so that as the wall moved south, she could observe her young officer at work, and soon their evening walks included the recently completed portion of the seawall. She could be seen almost every evening standing in the window of her upstairs bedroom waiting for the arrival of her suitor.

Many years after this event, the house burned. Around 1887, another house almost the same was built on the site. Several families occupied the house over the next few years during which frequent sightings of what appeared to be a young lady in 18th century dress was seen roaming around the house.

In more recent decades, the house has been a series of restaurants. Staff at those restaurants consistently report hearing footsteps and seeing what appears to be a young lady. There have also been a few instances reported by customers. No one seems to have any idea who the lady is or was. Stories handed down by some locals seemed to leave little doubt that she is the Lieutenant's lady.

Some also report that on occasion, she can be seen standing in an upstairs window late at night gazing toward the seawall. Not coincidentally, stories have suggested that on moonlight nights, against the moon reflected silvery bay, two pale bluish forms can be seen strolling the wall. Often a third form is trailing behind them. It is believed that this person was either the lady's mother or father chaperoning the couple, which was the accepted custom of that era.

The Lieutenant, owing to the grumblings of locals for his efforts on the wall rather than the directed fort repair, was replaced. The wall, however, was continued and completed in 1842, 3 feet in width, as the young Lieutenant had started.

So, should you encounter the couple on the wall, you should yield right of way because the couple apparently walks with a sense of ownership and entitlement. And well they should.

Exactly why the Lieutenant took it upon himself to redirect army funds from the fort repair to build the wall is unknown. As a federal officer, he had to know such a bold and reckless act would not help his career. Did he truly feel so strongly about the necessity of a wall to protect the town that he blatantly disobeyed orders? Or was he so smitten by his love that he followed his heart? It seems unlikely that he would have been allowed to remain assigned in Saint Augustine after his relief, but we don't know. Neither do we know what became of the young lady. Perhaps they married or perhaps he did leave and has now returned in spirit to be with his lady.

Chapter Sixteen

Honeyman and the Mermaid

The Saint Johns River, a few miles west of Saint Augustine, meanders 310 miles. It flows south to north -backwards- one of only two rivers in the world that does that. It is spring fed from the south and empties into the Atlantic Ocean northeast of Jacksonville. Because of its connection to the ocean, it is neither fresh nor saltwater but rather what is called brackish. It is home to a variety of fresh and saltwater fish, both finned and shelled. Blue Crabs abound and shrimp come into the river annually from the Atlantic. There are several ocean creatures who visit.

Except for storms in the semi tropical climate, the winds are a gentle breeze gusting higher in late afternoons. The tops of taller Cypress trees sway in the rhythm of the gusts. Cypress, the ancient guardians of the swamp, are uniquely formed; slender, irregular trunks, small, almost delicate appearing limbs and evergreen type needles rather than leaves enhance its graceful wind dance. The smallish limbs are probably a key part of nature's design, built to splinter in storm winds so they don't provide swaying leverage that could crack the trunk further down or uproot the tree from its foundation of mud, a requirement for good Cypress growth.

For centuries, the river had hosted several indian tribes, smuggler's, steam cargo and passenger vessels as well as modern barges. Sport and commercial fishing thrive. With the cauldron of activities for so many years, river stories abound.

One such story is the occasional sighting of a very large fish. The tail is described as three or four feet in width and when it breaks the top of the water, its' width is horizontal with the water as opposed to vertical, like fish. Only the tail has been seen so there is much speculation as to what it is. The one person who knows the identity of the creature never revealed his information except to selected family, and then only after swearing them to secrecy to protect the creature. I was privileged to hear the story from Honeyman when I met him some fifty plus years ago, and subsequently married his granddaughter.

Alfred Moseley, known to all as Honeyman, came to the Palmo Cove part of the River in the late 1800s on a cattle drive which he joined in northern Georgia at the age of twelve. He spent the rest of his long life on the river and the variety of work skills he developed was remarkable. They included: raising cattle, both dairy and beef; building docks, bulkheads, houses; building and running Palmo Fish Camp with cabins for fishermen and vacationing families. He even engineered a moonshine still during prohibition days and beyond, supplying a quality liquor for family and profit. Honeyman was an accomplished hunter and trapper (lots of alligators); beekeeper, which caused him to be affectionately named as Honeyman; and of course, his first love, commercial fishing and crabbing out of an old, sturdy 16-foot wooden boat he built.

Honeyman was loved by all who knew him. A small, wiry man; weathered by days spent working on the river and very strong from his many labors. He was a man of few words who would help anyone, anytime, and in any fashion. Acts which he clearly enjoyed. He was not a man to embellish, try to impress, or tell tall tales. Because of that, I was amazed to hear of this incident because it is so incredible.

Honeyman's strange encounter occurred in the 1930s. Economically, times were very hard. More fortunate were those on the river who grew produce and fished, hunted and trapped. Honeyman was very good at all those skills and made a habit of sharing his food with his city friends in Saint Augustine. On this day, he was working his trotline, catching channel catfish to take into town. As always, he was enjoying his early morning on the river as he pulled the boat along with the trot line, removed fish and rebaited. He saw a large swirl to his front left, perhaps

40 feet away. He continued working on his line, and as he moved closer, he could see the swirl was a manatee.

Honeyman loved these gentle creatures. Not a fish at all, but rather a mammal. Of the three types of manatees, those found in Florida are West Indian. They are very slow moving and spend a large amount of time grazing on river vegetation. Folks often call them sea cows and they can grow to 10 feet in length and weigh up to 2000 pounds. They are totally non- aggressive, but in the water, when they are playing, one needs to be wary of their size. They stick their head up briefly every 20 minutes or so to breathe. Manatees are warm blooded just as we are and nurse their babies with milk for one to two years. When they're born, either head or tail first, the calf weighs about 60 pounds and their lifespan can reach, and perhaps exceed, 70 years.

Honeyman had gotten about 10 feet from the manatee and could see that it seemed to be in distress. Its head broke the surface and it produced a high shriek. Honeyman dropped his line and paddled to the mammal. He immediately saw the problem.

The poor beast was tangled in a cast net, perhaps inadvertently netted by a shrimper or more likely, was foraging and hit the stray net. In any event, the net, torn in several places covered a large portion of the creature, including its broad tail.

Honeyman eased the boat alongside the struggling beast and grabbed a section of the net. He held the net in one hand, his knuckles touching the manatee's leathery skin. Careful not to get his hand caught in the net, he spoke to the manatee. It raised its head again, looked at him with dark, beautiful eyes and calmed its' struggling.

With his free hand, Honeyman took his knife from its sheath and began cutting the net. Sensing that she was being helped, the manatee lay perfectly still.

Struggling with the net, Honeyman could not get to a tangled mess around her tail. It was going to be necessary to get into the water so he could get under her to free the net. He looked around. No one was in sight. He was on his own. Without hesitation, he lowered himself over the side of the boat. He was not frightened but hoped she would remain calm and not thrust her several hundred-pound body against him.

He released the side of the boat with his free hand, knife clutched in the other and gently tapped the top of her head. She made a low noise and remained still. Honeyman lowered himself under the cold water, about ten feet deep. From her underside, he began working to free her tail from the net, careful not to cut the manatee.

Honeyman had to come up for air four

times, but finally he freed the net from the creature's tail. Exhausted, he clung to the side of the boat. This was a very high sided boat, made so to handle rough water. He tried to pull himself up but only succeeded in dropping his knife into the river. He held on, catching his breath for another attempt. Again, he failed. The manatee had turned and was looking directly at him. She made what he described as a squeaking noise, then a chirp, and disappeared under the water.

A few seconds passed, and Honeyman felt something under his feet. Too far out to be a gator. He moved his legs and felt pressure against the bottom of his foot. He felt along the object with his other foot and could feel it move up. He stiffened his knees and started rising as if something was lifting him, or he was standing on an object moving up; he wasn't sure which.

Honeyman chose not to question his good fortune, and as he reached a height that allowed him to lean his upper body over the side and into the boat, he threw his legs over and rolled onto the boat floor. He caught his breath and peered over the side of the boat to see if the manatee had anything to do with his rescue. A foolish thought, but something had helped. Sure enough, there was the manatee, barely submerged under the water. As Honeyman stared, her head seemed to be transforming. It took on an almost woman like face, though somehow different. He could see very high cheekbones, and a small elongated nose with tiny vertical nostrils. Something, hair like, but coarser, moved around her head with the water action. Though he could not see clearly in the dark river water, he could tell it was not a manatee head, and the face resembled a woman more than anything else he could think of.

The creature was facing him and leaned back as if to float, but then it rolled to its left. He caught sight of a paw or web like hand when it slid down her body as her roll was completed. She dove, and a large tail, perhaps three or four feet wide broke the surface and disappeared in a powerful thrust.

Honeyman was familiar with the sailor stories telling of mermaids, but he also knew that most attributed those sightings as manatees mistaken for the elusive magical creatures.

Honeyman asked himself many times over the years if he saw a mermaid, who helped him, or really a smart manatee repaying him. His belief was that they were one and the same.

Chapter Seventeen

The House on Bridge Street

Tenured residents of Lincolnville say that Ruth Masters, in life, refused to leave her beautiful house on Bridge Street. Her ghost continues to roam the premises a century later, though for many years, after the arrival of Isobel Sanchez, she became less restless and perhaps more accepting.

In the 1970's, Isobel Sanchez, an attractive, middle aged lady from New England decided to visit Saint Augustine. Isobel was a well-educated businesswoman who earned her fortune in the world of advertising. Recognizing the stressful demands of her profession, she sought a much-needed break, and because of her Spanish ancestry, picked the nation's oldest city, founded by the Spanish, for her retreat.

As she toured the town, discovering its amazing history, and enjoying the endless social activity, she realized that she didn't want to leave. Isobel was a very independent woman who had never married, had little family and no attachments, so the decision to retire and relocate was hers alone. She traveled back to New England to tie up loose ends and returned to

Saint Augustine to begin house hunting.

She knew she wanted to be in the city's heart and her realtor arranged several showings in that area, but she couldn't seem to find the right house. The realtor, growing weary, suggested she might want to purchase one of the old homes located around town and renovate to her liking. She agreed to that as a possibility and they began her search, without success until she noticed an old house on Bridge Street bordering Lincolnville. The sprawling old, two story Victorian house was obviously vacant and in need of much work. It was listed by another real estate company as an "as is" sale, so she arranged to meet one of their realtors on site.

The following day she entered the house with the young lady from the realtor's office to very dusty, cobwebbed surroundings. Several pieces of furniture were still present, covered with dust. Isobel asked the realtor why her company had chosen not to repair or at least clean the house better? She replied that it had been on the market for a long time, and some potential buyers had heard stories that the house was haunted and lost interest. She added that a good deal could probably be had. As a businesswoman the idea intrigued Isobel, and in her well-educated mind, the idea of ghosts was ridiculous.

Isobel and the realtor walked around, peering into the various rooms. Approaching the kitchen area, they heard the clinking of glasses. Exchanging glances, they entered the kitchen, where everything seemed to be in order, notwithstanding the mess from several years of neglect.

The two women left the kitchen to go upstairs, and as they approached the staircase, the stairs seemed to be creaking, as if someone was preceding them up the once elaborate oak boards. The young realtor was becoming nervous, but they continued to the top landing. As Isobel turned toward the first room, she heard a gasp behind her and turned to see the young lady with a terrified look on her face. When asked if she was feeling ill, the realtor stammered that something had touched her shoulder. Isobel told her it was probably just a bug and suggested she wait downstairs, to which she readily agreed. Isobel did admit to herself that it felt as though someone was watching her but attributed that to the large, quiet openness of the house.

Isobel continued the tour on her own without further incident and told the realtor she was interested but wanted to investigate the house and area history. The young lady, excited about the possibility of selling a house no one else had been able to, offered her complete assistance and suggested they leave.

Bridge Street is the northern border of a downtown area called Lincolnville, which was first settled in the 1860s by a few black squatters. When black slaves were freed after the civil war many more moved into the area known as the Africa District. Though located in the small downtown area, it was very separate from the mainstream for many years. Black residents farmed, started their own churches and some businesses. Most of the houses built in the district over the following century were small, simple frame dwellings. Isobel's house, like others along Bridge Street, was the exception.

The house was built in the late 1800s by one of the wealthy entrepreneurs of the Henry Flagler era. He invested in property, as well as several businesses and to the surprise of many, soon married a local common girl far below his own social station in life. Ruth was 30 years his junior, actually worked in one of his shops and was of course, elated over her good fortune. She fell in love with the house on Bridge St., considerably more elegant and much larger than the three-room dwelling she shared with her parents outside of town. Her new husband traveled frequently, and she was perfectly happy enjoying her new surroundings.

On one of her husband's many trips up North, he mysteriously died. Ruth mourned her husband and received many condolences from her new affluent friends but was comforted by the knowledge that the wonderful house was now all hers, along with his wealth. But this was not to be.

Her husband had failed to reveal that he had a wife and children up North. Owing no doubt to the other wife's social standing and own wealth, she was the benefactor of his will for all holdings including the house. During the bitter fight it was also revealed that her husband had been supporting a black mistress in Lincolnville. Ruth plunged from the height of happiness to shame and despair.

Inevitably, the Sheriff arrived with an eviction notice, stating Ruth had to leave, and the house was to be sold. Ruth refused to leave, and when the Sheriff and deputy sought to physically remove her, she ran up the stairs, looked down and yelled that she would never leave. She threw herself over the banister and was killed instantly.

The house was sold a few times over the years, but each time the occupants would leave citing "strange occurrences", until finally there were no prospective buyers. That is until Isobel arrived.

Undeterred by the history of the house, Isobel decided she wanted it. In her nonbelieving mind, she viewed the haunting stories as good fortune because of the discounted price, and she turned her attention to the renovation project. She enlisted three contractors, the first of whom was to repair the front porch and downstairs ceiling.

The contractor began work on the front porch and Isobel secured temporary lodging until the house was brought to a livable state. On the second day of work, she received a call from the contractor who wanted to know if anyone was in the house. She replied no. He stated that he kept hearing footsteps from inside, but the door was locked, and he couldn't get in to investigate. Because he was ready to start the inside ceiling work, she agreed to meet him there the next day with the key.

They entered the house, and everything seemed to be in place, so the contractor put his tools inside and set up ladders, with a plan of commencing work the following day.

When Bill, the contractor entered the next day, he immediately experienced a chill, causing his skin to tingle. Shrugging this off, he grabbed his tools and climbed the ladder to begin the ceiling work. After a few minutes he felt his ladder move slightly. He climbed down to ensure the feet were secured. They were. He started up the ladder again and it began moving away from the wall, as if someone was pushing it away. Dumbfounded, he backed down and repositioned the ladder, leaving his hammer and scraper on the fireplace mantle. He climbed up again and reached for his scraper but before his hand touched it, both it and the hammer fell to the floor.

Now, more than a little shaken, he

backed down the ladder again. As his foot hit the last rung and he prepared to step off, something pushed against his back. Instinctively jumping, both he and the ladder crashed to the floor. Uninjured, he struggled up, but the sound of a very low giggle stopped him. He could hear soft footsteps coming toward him. He felt very chilled, then something touched his arm.

When Isobel received Bill's call stating he would not be returning to the house, she was angry. They did, after all, have a contract. He explained what happened. After much cajoling, he agreed to return, but only if someone were with him while he worked. Isobel agreed, deciding to clean up an upstairs room and move in.

Isobel arrived at the house just before dark with her belongings. She found Bill's tools and ladders scattered around the floor but otherwise, nothing unusual. She began carrying her bags upstairs, and during each trip, she once again felt that something was watching her. With the last bag deposited, she entered the upstairs bathroom to wash her face, but before she could turn the water on, it started pouring out. The old-style sinks had two separate faucets, one for hot, one for cold. They started coming on and off alternating; cold, then hot, and so on.

Pondering the situation, but calm, she watched in fascination as the dim image of a young lady seemed to appear in the mirror over the sink. What felt like a hand touched her shoulder gently. She turned, but no one was there. She took a deep breath and started washing her hands in the still running water. As she reached for the hand towel hanging from its rack, it lifted and draped over her hands. Still, amazingly, undeterred, she began drying her hands. A barely audible voice said, "I won't leave my house."

Isobel finished drying her hands and hung the towel back, all the while contemplating this situation.

Suddenly, her decision made, she stated, "Fine. We will live here together." The water stopped and the air seemed to lighten.

Isobel finished her house and lived there for many years until her death. She was seen often in the early evening swinging in her front porch swing and occasionally, there seemed to be a young lady sitting next to her. It is reported that it's hard to tell, because for some reason the young lady seemed only barely visible.

The house is still occupied, though there have been several owners and renters. Ruth is still seen on occasion, though usually between occupants, when the house is vacant. Nearby Lincolnville residents seem to view this situation as normal, but the revolving door of occupants obviously do not.

137

Chapter Eighteen

Honeyman's Moonshine Still

In the late 1920s, deep in the thick swamps of Jack Wright Island, just west of Saint Augustine, the morning calm was broken by the baying of hounds and the noise made by five men stomping through the muck and thick growth.

The local man handling the dogs and a local deputy were reluctant participants in the affair. The other three men were federal agents, revenuers, in search of a moonshine still which a tipster had said was in this area. It was these men, unaccustomed to moving through thick woods and swamps who were making all the noise. They didn't really care that the moonshiners might be alerted because their intent was to find and destroy the still.

It had not been easy for the Feds to convince the two locals to guide them into this area of the swamp because as locals told it, strange things happened there, particularly, around the area where Indian Charles, a robber and highway man and his two half wolf dogs were killed by authorities. The local deputy had suggested other areas to look, but the Feds would not be dissuaded, and as a deputy, he had no choice.

The dog handler had refused to participate, as was his right as a civilian, but the Feds increased his compensation until he reluctantly agreed.

Through the thick Cypress trees, the men could finally see the remains of the swamp hut and previous hideout of Indian Charles. The still was suspected to be just behind the hut.

As they approached, it became very still. The slight breeze died, and it was perfectly calm. Birds, bugs, and other creatures of the swamp had stopped their chatter. Nothing moved. As the men moved closer, the dogs started a low growl, then stopped in their tracks. The curses and urging of their handler could not move them forward. The Feds chuckled, but the deputy was getting very nervous.

They stepped into the partial clearing where Charles had been hanged, and as they did so the leaves under the hanging limb began to rustle and rise in the air. The men froze as a translucent apparition, wavering and fading in and out in the early morning light, began to form. Behind the apparition could be heard a deep, vicious, low growling.

The two tracking hounds started whimpering and took cover behind the legs of their handler, who was holding their leashes tightly, standing frozen as he stared at the site before him.

One of the Feds gathered his wits enough

to pull his pistol and fire as he retreated backwards. Suddenly the air became frigid, the form seemed to grow larger and fade in and out in a more animated fashion. Now the growl behind the apparition took the wavering form of a very large dog or wolf. Its' snarls and growls grew deafening. A rusty knife embedded in a nearby tree, said to have been thrown at one of the locals capturing Charles years earlier started quivering as if trying to free itself.

The hounds broke free of their handler and fled the scene with their master in hot pursuit, happy to have an excuse to leave. The deputy shouted at the Feds to follow him and fled, with the Feds close behind.

The hunt for the still was abandoned. The Feds, after what they had witnessed and aware that all locals were familiar with the Indian Charles story, believed no one in their right mind would try to install a still in that area. They did not include the incident in their report, but it did become another part of the Indian Charles legend.

But there is a back story.

Alfred "Honeyman" Mosley, who had been in these parts since the late 1800s was the owner of the still, which in fact was there.

Honeyman was well known and well liked. He was a man who could seemingly do anything. He fished, crabbed, built docks, barns, houses; worked cattle, and had large beehives from which he had gotten the nickname Honeyman. Most important, he made the best moonshine around.

Moonshining in this era, prohibition, and in the sparsely populated rural areas was tolerated by the local law, many of whom were said to be compensated with money or product from the moonshiners. It was a mutually beneficial arrangement. Every so often, however, the Feds would show up, so all the deals were put on hold. Usually, the local law wouldn't reveal the location of stills, but the Feds had deep pockets and inevitably someone would provide information. These folks were branded traitors of the worst sort.

Honeyman's still at the time was located on the other side of the swamp from the Indian Charles site. He enjoyed a thriving business, delivering his shine throughout a wide area, including Saint Augustine and by river to Jacksonville. This changed when the Feds showed up and somehow managed to find his still.

As was the habit back then, they would plant dynamite around the still, invite members of the press with their photographers, then blow the still into another world.

Fortunately, Honeyman was not around when they found the still, nor could they prove it was his, so he escaped jail. But he did need another site to continue his business. It occurred to him that there was an area in the swamps said to be haunted where locals would not venture, and outsiders couldn't find it on a good day. He had never gone to that area because he never had a reason to do so. He was neither a believer nor a nonbeliever when it came to all the strange stories, though he had experienced unusual happenings along the river in other areas. He simply accepted the events and didn't really search for an explanation. He decided to scout the Indian Charles site.

Soon after the Feds had left and things returned to normal, Honeyman headed to the area. He went by boat, which took much longer but also lessened the chances of being seen. He maneuvered his boat out of the river and into the shallow swamp edge and tied it out of sight. He headed in the general direction of where he thought the Indian Charles site might be, based on stories and descriptions he had heard. Though he had to backtrack one time, sure he had overshot the site, he eventually could see what had to be the old swamp hut through the brush. He calculated, after subtracting time wasted due to the backtrack, that it wouldn't be too bad getting in and out to tend his still.

His plan would be to simply camp on site when cooking the shine rather than come and go, then haul his goods out when he had a nice load. He proceeded toward the hut to determine the ideal location for his equipment.

Honeyman stepped into the small clearing in front of the hut and became aware that all swamps sounds had stopped. He paused to take in the surroundings. The hut was rotten and falling in. He could see the big limb where Indian Charles was apparently hanged. The remains of a crude hitching rail lay just in front of the hut. Several feet to the left of the rail he could make out a small hole, partially filled with swamp debris. Near the hole he could see an old shovel, it's spade rusty and the handle broken and rotten.

He moved forward again, surrounded by silence but stopped when he noticed the leaves directly under the huge hanging limb, rustling as if disturbed by wind. But there was no wind. He started forward again and the leaves and ground debris started rising, taking form. Suddenly, he was knocked to his back as if something had pushed him.

Raising to a sitting position, he could feel what he described as hot breath on his face, and he could hear a low snarl very near to his head. It was as if an unseen animal had knocked him down and was now standing over him growling.

A man not easily scared, Honeyman decided if he were going to use this area, a deal would have to be made. He started talking as if someone else was present, which presumably, in some form, was the case.

He presented his plan, as if casually speaking to a prospective partner. He said he did not intend to disrupt or disturb Charles, nor was he interested in the treasure alleged to be buried there. His intent was only to pass through to erect a moonshine still and haul the shine out every so often. Since the activity was illegal, Honeyman would keep his activity and the location secret. He added that since Charles had been a robber and highway man, he could appreciate the need for a secure hideout.

The form that had started rising, began dropping to the ground. The growling stopped, and it felt as though the hot air moved away from his face. He stood. Nothing happened, so he moved forward to where the form had been. The leaves moved slightly, as if to acknowledge his presence. He walked on through to an area behind the hut where he determined it would be simple to erect his still.

Honeyman took a breath and headed back through the site. He passed through without incident except when he noticed the knife sticking in a tree and stopped, gazing at its long rusty blade and carved bone handle. The leaves behind him rustled slightly. Honeyman took that as a don't touch. He didn't.

Some months later, after several shine cookings and deliveries, the Feds entered the

area on a hunch. But then you've heard that story.

Chapter Nineteen

Ned's Friends

Several years ago, having finally secured a seat in the Bunnery on Saint George street, I sat down to enjoy a morning cup of coffee. The seating arrangement is such that my two-seater table was situated in the middle of the floor, about three feet from a booth directly to my right. It is a cozy arrangement, but space does not allow for a more spread out plan.

There were four middle aged tourists sitting in the booth, and I could easily hear their conversation. One couple was describing an incident that had happened to them the previous evening. They had enjoyed an outing at A1A Ale works on the Bayfront, so much in fact, they stayed until closing. Strolling back to their lodging located at the north end of Saint George street, they were enjoying the quiet deserted route they took. Suddenly, from the shadows, they heard low voices. They stopped to locate the source and could now also hear what sounded like several conversations taking place and the occasional laugh of a woman. Nothing could be seen. There were no lights in the two or three nearby buildings or anything else to suggest the sound was coming from those dwellings.

Quite suddenly, the voices stopped, as if the couple's presence had been discovered. They waited a moment, then hurried on to their inn, glancing back to an empty street as they went.

The couple seated with them politely pointed out that they had been drinking and sounds tend to carry in certain environments. While readily acknowledging both facts, the storytellers were adamant about what they had heard. They insisted the sounds were very near them and were not projected from outside their immediate location.

My curiosity aroused, I asked their forgiveness for intruding; introduced myself as a local; and expressed my interest in their story. Fortunately, they were very polite and asked if I had ever encountered such an event. To my inquiry as to the exact location of their experience, they replied that they were on the next street over, behind Colombia's Restaurant and at the intersection of another small street where an empty lot was located. The voices came from that lot.

I advised that the area described was the corner of Spanish and Cuna streets. They replied that that sounded correct. I told them that there were many such events reported throughout the Old Town, though I had not heard of any in that area, which was not to say there weren't any. We exchanged pleasantries for a few more minutes, and I took my leave.

My quick research revealed that the earliest property record of the lot in question was 1763. It was probably occupied long before that because its location was in the oldest area of the original settlement. The 1763 record listed Manuel Jacinto as the owner. He lived in what was described as a "house of board". Not much is known about Jacinto.

Sometime around 1777, Pablo Sabata and his family lived on the site in a wood structure with a thatched roof, not uncommon in that era. He owned the property until the mid-1800s.

In the late 1700s, an L shaped two room building was constructed on this site. In subsequent archaeology digs, broken tumblers and mug fragments were found, as well as over 100 pieces of pipe fragments, suggesting that the building or part of it was used as a tavern. In that era, it was not uncommon for a tavern owner to live on site. A major pastime for locals then was patronizing the local tavern frequently.

From the mid to late 1800s, it is unclear who owned the property, but in 1885 a two-story frame dwelling was built as a rental house for the working class. It was subsequently purchased in 1931 by "Dixie Canova" and his wife Estelle. Canova was a businessman and suspected bootlegger during prohibition. The house was demolished not long after his death in 1969, and the Saint Augustine foundation purchased the lot in 1978. Excavations at the site revealed four structures dating to the 1600s.

Still curious about the tourist couple's story, I called my longtime friend Ray, a well- known tour guide and "unofficial historian". He was also an information source for those involved in ghost tours and as such picked up stories about unusual happenings. In this case he did have information but from an unexpected source.

Ray asked if I remembered Ned, the homeless man. I did because Ned was unusual. There are more than a few homeless folks in Saint Augustine, and why not? The weather is accommodating, there are many overhangs, covered patios, and walkways as well as areas owned by the city, all offering shelter during rain. Tourists are usually free with a few coins and in a pinch, the Saint Francis House is good for free meals and a cot.

As I mentioned, Ned was not your 'run of the mill' homeless person. He was an educated man whose age was hard to determine. He had a pleasant way about him, relaxed: Ned had simply "dropped out." For many years, he had lived on the streets of the Old Town and was well known and liked.

My friend Ray routinely walked on Spanish Street to pick up tour groups at the Visitor Information Center. He became well acquainted with

Ned since they encountered each other many times. Ray found the man to be very interesting. Approaching the vacant lot in question one morning, he saw Ned climbing the fence to exit the rear corner of the lot. Ray stopped and Ned approached him with his usual 'good morning'.

They exchanged pleasantries and Ray offered him a couple of bucks before he left, which Ned declined, as he usually did. Ned put his pack on his shoulders and with a smile asked that Ray not tell his tourist friends about his companions in the lot because it was his favorite sleeping place on nice nights. He explained he didn't want to be bothered by a bunch of 'gawkers'. He added that the other vagabonds didn't bother him because they were afraid of his friends.

Ray asked him who he was referring to and Ned replied that he would tell him if he would keep his secret. Ray assured him that he would. Now, since Ned had left a couple years prior, Ray agreed to tell me Ned's story concerning the lot.

Seems that Ned told him that on many occasions at night he had heard conversations while at the back corner of the lot. He couldn't understand all that was said because it was always somewhat subdued. He did figure out over time, that it was probably former patrons of the tavern. He added that he didn't mind because they left him alone and he left them alone. Ray could tell that the old gentleman was serious. He told Ned his secret was safe with him and departed.

The next day, Ray finished a tour and was headed for his car. He exchanged hellos, as he had done many times, with the elderly lady who lived in the house next to the lot. He knew that the old lady spent a great deal of time on her porch, so he asked her if she ever noticed anything unusual at the lot next door. She commented that she knew Ned snuck in there to sleep on occasion. She added that of course there was the comings and goings of the tavern folks. Ray asked what she meant. She said rather matter of factly that there had been a tavern there many years back, and sometimes at night she could see the shadowy figures of people disappearing right through the fence. She could also hear them from the porch some nights. She added that Ned sees and hears them because they had talked about it. Ray asked if these events bothered her and she replied not at all because she just 'let them be'. "A good idea, don't you think?" she said to Ray. He agreed.

Chapter Twenty

Revenge

Poltergeist, as most of us recall from the popular movie of the same name, is a ghost that is more active than your "normal" ghost. The term is centuries old, apparently coined in Germany and literally means "noisy ghost".

Scenarios associated with a poltergeist seem to be centered around sudden physical events such as objects mysteriously moving, falling, flying on their own accompanied by lots of loud noise. Generally, the creation of havoc and terror.

Sometimes referred to as "mischievous spirits", because they like to gang up on the living; they seem to plan their activity for maximum chaos. Some experts say that the poltergeist experience is often tied to a person who has experienced extreme stress or frustration over a period of time, suggesting the person may in fact be the cause of an encounter.

The poltergeists rarely present as a visual apparition, but when they do, they are generally distorted, or even monstrous. Experts seem to agree that they can change locations, and most cases only last a few weeks or months. Personally, I have only been told one story that would fit into the poltergeist category.

Joan is a lady of about 40 years old from the Midwest who was the victim of an extremely abusive husband. He had experienced many extended stays in jail, usually having to do with alcohol and drugs. After many years of mental and physical abuse, Joan finally filed for divorce from this very dangerous individual. Upon learning what Joan had done, her husband beat her severely, for which he was once again jailed.

While her ex was in jail, Joan decided to make her break by leaving town, advising only her mother of her whereabouts and only after being assured her location would be kept secret. She picked Saint Augustine as her new home because of a previous visit she enjoyed.

Joan quickly found a job and a small rental house in the old part of Vilano Beach, next door to Saint Augustine. Within days of moving in, her mother phoned to tell her that her ex-husband had been killed trying to escape jail. Apparently, when he learned she had left, he became so enraged, he tried to overpower the guards and lost his life in the process. Both sad and relieved, Joan decided to put it all behind her and get on with her life.

Several weeks had passed when Joan arrived home from work one day to find both the television and the radio on. Thinking she had been forgetful, she turned both off and went to the kitchen to prepare dinner. As she stepped into the kitchen, the television came on again. She turned to go check that situation, but as she did, a drinking glass flew off the table and struck her in the back. Though frightened, she composed herself and preceded to the television which now was flipping through channels without assistance. She turned it off and returned to the kitchen where everything seemed normal.

A couple of days later, Joan woke from what she thought was a bad dream to find her bed violently shaking. It was as if someone had lifted the foot of the bed and was shaking it. She jumped from the bed and turned the light on, only to find an empty room and the bed perfectly still. Badly shaken, she spent the remainder of the night in a chair in the living room. After very little sleep, she was startled awake by the television blaring, again flipping through channels.

Things were quiet for a few days, then a frightening incident happened. Arriving home from a long day at work, she decided to have a hot bath. She lit an incense candle at the foot of the bathtub and lowered herself into the warm water. As she felt the day's stress leave her body, something touched the top of her head. Alarmed, she jerked her head forward, but something pushed her under the water. Struggling, the pressure on her head released, and she gulped for air as a voice said vehemently, "bitch"! She subsequently insisted the voice was her ex- husband's.

As a devoted Roman Catholic, Joan sought help from the priest of a local church she had been attending. He said he would be happy to pay a visit and bless the house.

The priest arrived and Joan opened the door, but as he tried to enter, the door slammed in his face knocking him backwards. In Joan's words, "if he had not believed my story before, he did now!"

Undeterred, the priest re-entered and set about performing some type of blessing designed to rid a place of evil spirits. He completed this task, and as he was about to leave, he took Joan's hand and told her that he was sorry, but he could still feel a presence in her house.

It was at this point that I met Joan, who had sought me out during a book signing event. Since I am by no means an expert in this field, I put her in touch with a retired professor friend of mine who had done extensive research in the paranormal field. He visited twice, learned as many details as he could and finally told her that if she felt she could endure it, she should "ride it out." His logic was that in these type cases, there was the possibility the house was not the problem. He went on to explain that if it was a spirit targeting her, leaving would probably have no effect because it would simply follow her. He reassured her that he knew of no case that involved loss of life or serious injury, and that almost always the ordeal ended when the victim confronted her tormentor.

There were a few more incidents over the following few weeks. None were as violent or traumatic as the bathtub incident. She claimed to have heard his voice again, prompting her to throw the remote control in that direction. She also would arrive home and find something in disarray, such as overturned furniture, broken dishes, and the television on. Something touched her on one other occasion but not forcibly. Then, as the professor had suggested, things became normal.

When I last heard from Joan, everything was still quiet, and she was finally starting to enjoy her new home and the Old Town.

Chapter Twenty-One
Tinaja

Most have heard the story of Ponce de Leon's discovery of Florida and his belief in the so-called Fountain of Youth. Water from the fountain was reputed to have magical powers because it offered a longer life for those who drank from the fountain. A related story suggests Ponce and others through the years were instead looking for an ancient artifact, some type of drinking vessel, which when drunk from, extended one's life. This vessel was first in the possession of a Timucua Indian Chief but later disappeared.

The chief who held the Tinaja, the Timucua word for drinking vessel, was killed in battle. At the time of his death, he was said to have lived three lifetimes because of the power of the Tinaja. It appears that while the Tinaja extended life, it did not protect against physical injury. Another side effect was that it also caused evil things to happen. The Timucua began referring to the Tinaja as hitiquiry; their word for demon or evil spirit because it changed their chief from a respected ruling chief to one feared by other tribes as well as his own. He evolved to rule by brutality and had a fondness for warring on his neighbors. Stories suggested that before each raid, the chief presided over a ceremony calling on the power of the Tinaja.

There is no description of the Tinaja other than the outline of an eagle feather carved on its surface. The feather was the mark of the chief. After the death of the chief, the new chief, one of his grandsons, took possession of the Tinaja. He proclaimed that because of his belief that the Tinaja was hitiquiry, neither he nor anyone else would drink from this vessel. Nevertheless, even though he did not drink from the Tinaja, he began having nightmares and visions of evil things and became concerned about its impact on his tribe. When he and others began seeing apparitions of his grandfather, many of his young warriors urged him to drink from the Tinaja, so he turned to a Spanish priest he had befriended for help.

The priest, Father Pareja, had arrived in the area in the mid-1600s and set about interacting with the local indians. In his mission to convert them to Christianity, he learned their language and began a journal about their culture and his efforts with them. In this role, he and the chief had many discussions and became friends, so when the chief turned to him for help, he had no qualms.

The priest was fascinated by the chief's story but of course, did not believe it, though he didn't reveal his feelings to his friend. The

Timucua were superstitious and that had to be considered when dealing with them. He assured the chief he would rid the Tinaja of its evil powers with his Christian rituals and put it in a safe place. He entered an accounting of this event in his journal.

Father Pareja was bitten by a water moccasin and died in the early 1700s; some sixty plus years after he was given the Tinaja. He would have been at least 100 years old but was described as forever young. His replacement, a friar by the name of Pineda arrived and was immediately beset with stories from his flock about some of his predecessor's strange behavior, much not in keeping with church norms. The young friar set about "mending fences", and things slowly returned to normal.

While performing housekeeping tasks in his modest lodgings, formerly Father Pareja's residence, Father Pineda discovered the Tinaja and journal. He had heard brief comments about this story and was curious to see it in his predecessor's journal. As a cautious man, he decided to bury the Tinaja under the floor of the settlement church in what is now downtown St. Augustine.

Father Pineda removed enough of the old wooden floorboards to allow a small hole to be dug. He prepared the hole, but as he picked up the Tinaja for burial, he felt a presence and the air around him felt chilled. When he saw a form start to materialize, he dropped the relic into the hole, grabbed his Bible and performed a type of exorcism.

The Tinaja would remain buried for centuries until about 1900 when an archeological dig in downtown St. Augustine occurred amidst some controversy. There were several people working the site and some reported seeing unusual things and hearing what was described as murmurings on occasions. There were also accusations that one of the team members, a Nathaniel Fuller, had not turned over all his finds, including some type of old, worn, leather-bound book and perhaps an artifact. With some embarrassment, one worker stated that an apparition, maybe indian, had appeared and all but one team member had fled the scene -- Fuller. Fuller, at the time in his late forties, denied the accusations but left the team. He remained in town, living in his small house just off Cordova Street where he continued his own work in the archeological arena, which included writing articles for various magazines.

Those on Fuller's former team were aware of the Tinaja story and based on one worker's glimpse of the missing artifact, suspected that Fuller had indeed taken the mysterious item when the others fled. Soon, one of the team members was shot and killed by Fuller while he was allegedly trying to rob Fuller's house. It seemed rather strange that a professional archeologist would be breaking into a house but, nevertheless, Fuller was not charged. Word of this event got out, as did the Tinaja story, and there were other burglary attempts, prompting Fuller to finally move.

A very young St. Augustine policeman working these cases found the entire affair intriguing. He didn't believe in apparitions but after interviewing Fuller on many occasions, was suspicious of the strange little man. However, even after several incidents and subsequent investigations, there was no evidence to charge him. Fuller now lived about 150 miles west of St Augustine in the Florida panhandle where he continued archeological digs and lectures on occasion. The young policeman kept tabs on Fuller through the police at Fuller's new home, but as things quieted down, eventually he stopped.

Some 70 years later, the policeman, now retired and well into his nineties was looking through the newspaper over morning coffee and noticed an article about an important indian site discovery in the panhandle. Curious, he began reading the article which continued on the next page, where there were pictures of the dig and the principal researchers.

One face caught his attention for some reason; the researcher's name was Professor Nolan. Then it hit him. He quickly dug out the old file he had kept concerning the missing artifact case years ago. He shuffled through the papers until he found the picture he wanted. Laying it beside the newspaper photo it was obvious that the photos were of the same man. Professor Nolan was Professor Fuller, but that was quite impossible! Nolan was not an old man and Fuller would have to be over 100 years old!

He studied the pictures with his magnifying glass and was convinced it was indeed Fuller. Under the powerful glass he could also barely make out something behind Fuller. His first thought was that it was due to poor newspaper quality, but then he realized it wasn't that at all. The image, pale, misty like, though dim and blurry, had human form! He recalled the stories and the accusations and realized with a chill, that the evidence was right before him.

Chapter Twenty-Two

The Phantom*

My good friend, Rex Schaafsma, told me this story and allowed me to edit and include it in this book.

If you are reading this story, you have found this note in a bottle written by myself or one of my compatriots. Our bottles are found in many places, perhaps the landfill, or floating in the park lake, and the notes are all the same because we are only allowed to tell our story as presented here. The story also contains specific instructions, on which the work of my friends and I depend.

All of you big folks ... that is what we call you... have in your house, condo, or apartment, a drawer that is not reserved for any one particular item of apparel or routine use items. You know the one I'm referring to. It contains a random collection of useful and not so useful items ... string, tape, scissors, old comics, Tom Mix decoder rings and many other things which you can't recall obtaining, some not easily identified as anything.

You big folk have such a fascination with these drawers that you give them pet names: the catchall drawer; the what-not drawer; the junk drawer; or maybe the stuff drawer.

We are stealthy in the dark of the night and full of tomfoolery. We make items in your drawer disappear. But we also place back in your drawer, new old items; you know, those you can't recall ever having. It's a joy! We live for it! Well, we don't really live, but we aren't ghosts; we really resent being viewed as ghosts (although some of you do have ghosts in your houses); we get along OK with them.

Now, for our efforts, we do sometimes snatch a cookie, or maybe a chicken leg. Personally, I am fond of cherry sodas. It's not much compensation for the pleasure we know you get trying to remember where those drawer items came from. Our biggest pleasure though, is taking things that you never miss, because you don't remember ever having them. That's the best part of a junk drawer ... you don't know what's there! Which brings me to the purpose of this note.

My friends and I were created long ago, about the time of some of our other mischievous acquaintances; leprechauns, tooth fairy, Easter Bunny, and so on. My clan is more ambitious than those "temps" because we work at our mischief constantly; unless we're caught. There's the rub!

You see, there is a clause in the deal with our creator that we never really bothered to worry about, knowing the habits of you big folk. The clause states that if one of you actually misses an item we take... and it has to be specific, i.e... you actually look for it... then we fold up into ourselves, never to prank again. I'm sorry, and ashamed to say that I am the culprit who has caused this.

Some time ago, I entered an unusually neat, landscaped home. That should've been a warning. Everything was in its proper place; so orderly, that anything amiss would surely be recognized by this overly proper big folk. Even the "drawer" was arranged so perfectly, I was taken back!

But it was too tempting. I took an item and replaced it with another.

Yeah, you guessed. The big folk in this case missed the item, demanded to know from other household members where the new one came from and wouldn't let it go.

Now, me and my kind have been folded up, but if you are reading this, you can release us; and you do need to release us because you need that drawer. You need to ponder the new stuff added which is not happening now. You need that old stuff to disappear before your drawer grows so heavy it collapses. But most of all, you need to help because I and my friends miss having fun in your drawer.

Here is all you have to do. Open your stuff drawer. Close your eyes. Say our name softly three times: Phantom, Phantom, Phantom. Now look into your drawer. See something you don't remember?

If so, thank you. We are enjoying a stretch and our fun filled adventures continue.

The Phantom

Chapter Twenty-Three

South of the Plaza

One of my favorite areas of Saint Augustine lies South of the Plaza. The Old Saint Augustine Village is certainly one of the more interesting places to visit, but the surrounding areas should not go unnoticed. This area, including the Village was depicted on the earliest town plans. The somewhat rough, bumpy streets, sprawling beautiful old homes, most of which have been renovated many times, and the general ambiance offers a sense of several centuries of life and history in the Old Town. During early morning or later evening strolls, when the day's activities have faded away, if you listen carefully and your senses will allow, you can hear and sense that history. Perhaps you'll detect the clop of horse's hooves, the squeaking of a wagon or cart, the subtle rattling of a soldier's sword or maybe even voices. As a frequent stroller through this area, I felt compelled to mention four sites together rather than in separate chapters. That is not to say that there aren't other places located in the south end that have their own story, but rather the four chosen have consistent reports of strange occurrences over the years. Strolling by those sites, as I often do, I always seem to experience unusual sensations. My senses just seemed to come alive. I believe I have even smelled bread from the building that was the Kings Bakery for Saint Francis Barracks during the British rule.

First Site: The Old St Augustine Village

The Old Saint Augustine village site was included on town plans dating back to at least 1572. Records suggest there was once a cemetery and a Spanish church on the grounds, as well as many other buildings, and most of the houses. Today there are nine buildings on the grounds. Most of the original buildings have been gone for many years. Those left generally span the time between 1790 and 1910. During this time, buildings were torn down, rebuilt, renovated, sold and resold until Kenneth Dow bought all nine buildings over a period of ten years beginning in the 1940s. He subsequently donated it all to the Daytona Museum of Arts and Sciences. Today of course, the buildings and antiquities can be enjoyed by all. With such a long history, it is not surprising that numerous reports of unusual happenings have been made.

A few years back, a paranormal research team visited the grounds and did in fact capture unusual readings on their instruments, as well as orbs in photographs. The team also reported that while upstairs in one of the houses, they heard footsteps in another room, and when they investigated, nothing or nobody was found.

Staff members have reported similar occurrences, and some have reported seeing the figure of a man and gates being opened by an unseen presence. With such a long history, how could there not be ghosts?!

Second Site: The Oldest House

To the South of the Village, and one block west, is the Oldest House. Talk about history! The oldest house is almost 300 years old and apparently has had only six owners, including the Saint Augustine Historical Society who purchased the home in 1918.

An artillery man and his wealthy wife built the basic house around 1723 and lived there for 46 years, raising 11 children, several of whom died before adulthood. In 1775, the British paymaster bought the house and added a second floor where a store and tavern catering to soldiers was installed. It was sold again in 1788. That family and their descendants lived in the house for almost 100 years. Dentist CP Carver bought the house in 1884 and it was under his ownership that it became known as "The Oldest House".

During that long history, there were many children born and raised in the house and perhaps even more deaths, natural, accidental, and otherwise. Certainly, there would have been thousands of family guests and patrons of the store and tavern. It is no wonder then that there have been reports of 'happenings' over the years. It is interesting to me that as far as I could determine, those happenings are not definitive. It seems to be more a matter of what people sense or feel; a presence, or subtle movement, or breeze, where there should be none, a caress when alone. Are the sounds heard, described as old rafters or beams shifting, real or imagined? Certainly, real to those who experience such things, but again not very definitive. Such is not the case with a neighboring area just down the street.

Third Site: Aviles Street

When one crosses King Street from the Plaza and enters Aviles Street under the old archway, there is a strong sense of old Saint Augustine. Much of the city's colonial character has been retained the entire length of the street, formally known as Hospital Street.

All manner of sightings, sounds, and experiences have been reported in and around the various buildings and throughout the street. Probably most originate from the site of the Spanish Military Hospital. First built in 1793 as a hospital and off and on livery stable, the present building is a replica of the original. The museum gives one a glimpse of wardrooms, mourning rooms and apothecary with its variety of herbs and medicines.

Many incidents of being touched, furniture and other items moving on their own, and apparition sightings have been reported. More than one paranormal investigation team has described unusual experiences.

Taken collectively, the sheer age and number of historic buildings, sites, and events on Aviles Street, creates an infinite possibility for hauntings.

The Ximenz-Fatio House was constructed in 1797 by Ximenz, a prominent merchant who operated his business and lived on the property. It was bought in 1855 by Louisa Fatio, a member of an old Florida family. For many years, it was a boarding house for distinguished visitors. Many of these were influential men from the North who made it their annual winter residence. Some, they say, can still be heard and occasionally seen wandering the grounds.

The O'Reilly house was built during the Second Spanish Period and was occupied for many years by Father Michael O'Reilly who came to Saint Augustine in 1785 and was instrumental in the construction of the Cathedral. He willed the house to the church on his death in 1812.

The Gaspar Papy House was built by one of the early Greek colonists who came to Saint Augustine from New Smyrna. Many tales surround this house.

The building currently used by the Saint Augustine Historical Society as a research library was built in 1813 as a Saint Augustine style colonial home. It was purchased by Joseph Smith, a federal judge. His son was the famous Confederate General Edmund Kirby-Smith, who grew up in the house and according to some, can still be heard playing in the courtyard. It was subsequently donated as a public library.

Others could be listed, but the point is that one cannot walk Aviles Street, the oldest in Saint Augustine, without a deep sense of history invading the soul. You may choose to take that walk late at night, or perhaps early in the morning hours to get a sense of other, hidden things: an unidentifiable noise; a fleeting shadow; a wisp of air across your face. Some sensations explainable; some, maybe not.

Fourth Site: Maria Sanchez Lake

I cannot write about the South end of town without mentioning Maria Sanchez Lake, shown on a very early town plan as Maria Sanchez Creek. As far as I can determine, Henry Flagler dammed the north end of the creek so he could fill in that area for building projects. But before the Spanish arrived, the creek, with access to the ocean, was a campsite for at least one tribe of indians, probably more.

I was told as a boy and more recently, by people living at that end, they, when on evening walks, or while peering out of windows, often saw pale images of dancing people. Smoke has been smelled when there were no fires in the area, and one very old lady, who lived near the south end of the creek insisted she routinely heard what she described as chanting.

In the hundreds, perhaps thousands of years Native Americans roamed this area before the Europeans arrived, how many camped on the banks of the creek? No doubt some were buried in its proximity and still gather there on occasion.

Chapter Twenty-Four

Other Unusual Happenings

St. Augustine Lighthouse

The present-day Saint Augustine lighthouse was built in 1872-1873 to take the place of an older coquina structure that was located a short distance northeast. The current lighthouse is an imposing, 165-foot-tall structure that boasts eight flights of spiral staircases with a total of 219 steps to the top.

There have been many reports of sightings and unusual occurrences regarding both the tower and the grounds, where the sound of giggling and footsteps have been heard, rumored to be the spirit children of a lighthouse keeper from years past.

The national TV show "Ghost Hunters" documented more than one strange occurrence, including a figure moving up the steps where no living person was located. The ghost of a man who hanged himself in the light keeper's house has been seen swinging from the rafters, and a light keeper who fell to his death many years ago is said to sometimes show up.

Castillo de San Marcos

The Castillo de San Marcos is the defining historic landmark of the Old Town. The original fort was very small and made of wood. Construction of the current structure began about 1672 and took two plus decades to complete.

Many stories are told about the ghosts of the Castillo, including Chief Osceola of the Seminole Indian tribe wandering the grounds searching for his head. Osceola was captured in 1837 and held in the fort, but was subsequently moved to Fort Moultrie, South Carolina, where he died, and Doctor Frederick Weeden allegedly severed his head from his body.

There are several ghost stories involving a previously unknown room found after a gun deck caved in during the early 1800s. Several things were found, including skeletons and shackles. Unusual sounds are often heard coming from that area.

Andrew Ransom

One of many pirates sailing the East Coast

in the 17th century was the Englishman Andrew Ransom.

Ransom was shipwrecked, and along with a dozen of his men, was captured by the Spanish. His men were given prison sentences, but Ransom was sentenced to die by garroting. The event was to be held in the Plaza, but as the stick garrote was turned to execute the sentence, the rope broke. The parish priest had noted during this event that Ransom held a Catholic rosary; unusual for a protestant Englishmen. Viewing the broken garrote as a sign, the priest put Ransom under the protection of the church.

Ransom was held in Saint Augustine 12 years, during which he proved very helpful in several town and church projects, including the Castillo construction. After that, he was freed.

Some say the ghost of Ransom still frequents the Plaza.

City Gates

Located at the north end of Saint George Street, the city gates were built around 1729, though the coquina pillars were added later, in 1808. Then, there were actual gates between the pillars, and they were closed and locked at curfew nightly.

Frequent reports from late night visitors to that area claim to have heard a young girl's voice and felt a light touch by someone or something unseen.

Many attributed these phenomena to a young girl, Lizzie, who reportedly missed curfew on a very cold night and perished outside the locked gates.

Harry's

The beautiful old building on the Bayfront that is currently Harry's restaurant was rebuilt to its current original design in 1888, after a fire razed the original home, built around 1750.

Catalina de Porras was one of nine children of the family who built the original house and lived there for about ten years, until the British took over Florida in 1763. Catalina and her family went to Cuba but returned in 1784 when the Spanish reclaimed Florida. Catalina subsequently reclaimed the house, where she died many years later.

After Catalina's death, the house changed hands numerous times, and in more modern times, it has been home to several restaurants. Throughout this time, there have been numerous reports from occupants, diners, and wait-staff regarding the ghosts of two people.

One, a lady in a long flowing dress, is thought to be Catalina. She is usually seen, or felt, upstairs and reflected in a mirror. No one seems to know who the other figure, a man, could be. Usually in black, he seems to stay downstairs, many times near the old fireplace. The fireplace has also been known to ignite itself!

Lieutenant Guillermo Delaney

It is said that a restless spirit is sometimes seen or heard on Charlotte Street near Treasury Street. If you are in that area late at night and feel a rush of cold air accompanied by a sensation that you are not alone, it could be that Lieutenant Delaney is making his presence known.
In 1785, Lieutenant Guillermo Delaney, a young Spanish officer assigned to the fort was in route to see his lady, a seamstress who lived with a family on Charlotte street. It was a cool November evening and as the officer neared his ladies' home, he was attacked by two hooded men and stabbed. He died of his wounds about two months later.

Two soldiers were jailed, apparently based only on the suspicion of the mistress. Though an investigation ensued, this was the early years of the Second Spanish Period and things were confused and hectic. There were no eyewitnesses and very little evidence, although it was revealed that one of the accused had also been seeing the seamstress. The men remained in prison without a trial for five years. At that point, the archives are not clear as to their disposition, but it appears they were freed.

Some feel that the young lieutenant remains restless, not having received justice for his murder and makes his presence known on occasion.

Oldest Wooden Schoolhouse

Employees at the oldest wooden schoolhouse tell me that over many years, unexplained sounds, movements, and sudden subtle changes of temperature in the building have been noted.

The house was built around the mid-1700s, but before that the site was an army barracks. In 1788, it became the first school in the new world, configured as you see it now; classroom downstairs and teacher's living quarters upstairs. The cookhouse was built away from the main building to avoid fire incidents.

On a personal note, I have been a guest author, signing books in this old building on several occasions. While I have not seen anything unusual, I have, during tourist lulls, when I am alone in the classroom, heard sounds that are not normal and felt a difference in the air. When tourists are present, even if relatively quiet, things feel normal. When they leave, and before others arrive, not so much. I can't really describe it, but the air is just not the same.

Ripley's

Ripley's Believe It or Not Museum is full of all manner of oddities and apparently that includes ghosts. Employees, and in some cases visitors, have reported having their hair touched and feeling a sensation of being watched. There have also been reports of hearing the moans and crying of a woman. Some attribute these happenings to the spirits of two women who died in the building years ago.

A close friend of Henry Flagler, William Warden, built the structure as a winter home in 1887. It subsequently sat empty for many years until the novelist Marjorie Kinnan Rawlings bought it in 1941 and turned it into a hotel. Three years later a fire broke out on the top two floors and two young women from Jacksonville died in the blaze. The building was bought by Ripley soon after.

For many years paranormal experiences like those described above have been reported by the employees. Most of those employees simply accept these encounters as normal, but some have sought other employment after such events. You might say perspective is everything!

Marine Street Murder

There is no better place to take a quiet evening stroll than on Marine Street and the narrow surrounding streets just south of the Florida National Guard Complex. While the ambience is uplifting, residents and visitors alike have reported that when passing the former home of Athalia Lindsey, on Marine Street, unusual sensations can be felt. In the words of one resident "Your vibes just seemed to change as you move past the property." Some attribute these experiences to the restless ghost of Athalia, perhaps still seeking justice for her murder.

Athalia Lindsey was a former New York model and dancer who moved into the house on Marine Street in 1972. A feud immediately developed between Athalia and one of her neighbors, Allen Stanford. The feud soon grew from simple differences over dog barking, garbage cans, and so on to attacks by Athalia of Stanford's competence as a county manager. She was extremely vocal, complaining at county meetings, in the newspaper, and face to face. The relationship became very bitter; so much so that threats were made, and on January 23, 1974, Athalia's partly decapitated body was found on the front steps of her residence.

Though the crime scene was not handled well by the local police, there was ample evidence discovered to implicate Stanford. He was charged with her murder.

The trial only lasted two weeks, and the jury deliberated a mere two hours before acquitting Stanford, despite substantial evidence. Athalia had been unpopular in town; even the newspaper referred to her in unflattering terms. Many felt her unpopularity had much to do with Stanford's acquittal, but in any event, it seems that justice was not served.

Out of respect for the current occupants, I will not reveal the address of Athalia's house on Marine Street, but should you choose to stroll that street, you may feel its location.

Robert Searles

In the early hours of the morning, while the Old Town sleeps, sit on a bench in the Plaza and listen to the history. Surrounded by the small, old streets and the bay, you can hear it. You may also hear the frightened voices of people running, but in vain as they meet their fate at the end of a cutlass or musket ball.

In 1667, a Spanish supply ship leaving

Saint Augustine was captured off the coast of Cuba by Jamaican privateers, led by the pirate Robert Searles. Informed by one of the captured crew that there was silver to be had in Saint Augustine, Searles sailed the supply ship back to Saint Augustine. When a launch was sent out to greet what everyone assumed to be the supply ship, the crew was captured and secured in the ship's hold.

Searles and 100 Pirates landed on the wharf below the Plaza, and while the town slept, captured the guardhouse and the silver loot. At the time, there were about 120 soldiers defending Saint Augustine, who led by their Sergeant Major, fled to the surrounding woods. This left Searles and his men free to run amuck, which they did, killing about 60 people in the streets and taking several prisoners to be sold as slaves. Thankfully Searles did not burn the town or capture the fort.

The noise of the mayhem and screams of the slaughtered can sometimes be heard in the stillness of the night as restless spirits move about in the Plaza.

Ghosts

Another Summer in the Old Town

What haunting mystery connects the OLD JAIL and TOLOMATO CEMETERY?

Determined to find the cause behind ghostly encounters three unsuspecting friends enter the realm of apparitions and poltergeists. In a race against time, they discover the secret that can release spirits trapped 'in-between'.

Randy Cribbs stirs these spirits, colorful local characters and young romance into a heart-warming mystery set against the backdrop of the Nation's Oldest City. *Ghosts is* the winner of 3 Book Awards, including the Royal Palm Literary Best Book Award.

The Vessel ... Tinaja

When the body of archaeologist William Stewart is found floating in St. Augustine Bay, a curious reporter finds himself caught up in a web of hideous secrets, deceit, and murder woven by the lure of the tinaja and its terrifying power.

At first his empirical mind refuses to believe the old Indian story. As he is drawn deeper into Stewart's past and his own deadly lover's triangle, each ghastly revelation points to an unimaginable power and moves him dangerously close to the line that separates right from wrong, fact from myth. Now that power may be within his grasp!

Was Ponce de Leon pursuing the wrong object for everlasting youth?

The Vessel...Tinaja is an Eric Hoffer Book Award Finalist and is being considered for a feature length film.

Tales from the Oldest City

Randy Cribbs affection for St. Augustine, the Nation's Oldest city and old Florida is evident in this colorful collection of short stories.

From the mystery of '*So Little Time*', and the adventure of '*Mike's Birds*' to the heartwarming '*Riverman*', humor of '*Peanuts*' and romance of '*Tattoo*', readers are presented with a broad variety of tales guaranteed to tickle the imagination.

Randy's ability to blend fact and fiction into entertaining stories makes this picturesque tour through the Old Town a special way to visit and revisit the unique places, history and colorful characters of Saint Augustine, the Saint Johns River and surrounding area.

One Summer in the Old Town

In this two-time Book Awards winner, Randy draws the reader into a summer adventure set in Saint Augustine and on the banks of the Saint Johns River. A well-researched, historical overview of the Nation's Oldest city is woven into the fast-paced story through a host of colorful characters. A great story and an interesting, fun way to learn about the history, landmarks, and mystique of the Old Town; it includes original drawings by artists Manila Clough.

Used by schools and book clubs throughout the region, this book is enjoyed by all ages. A reader's guide is also available on request.

Ancient City Treasures

Across the pages of this two-time award-winning book stride the places, characters and events of old Saint Augustine.

Vividly share your Old Town visit with friends and family through historical turn of the century drawings and the poetic narrative of Randy Cribbs.

Readers are transported through time to sensually experience the history, charm and mystique of the Nation's Oldest city.

Old St Augustine Through the Centuries

Multiple award-winning author Randy Cribbs thoughtful narrative, paired with antique images presents a vivid snapshot of the places, characters, events and mystique of old Saint Augustine: 450 years of history!

Just a Dog
And the Musings of his Pet

Smile, cry, laugh, understand ... an inspirational book of discovery for all who have shared life with their special pet.

To Murphy, rules were simply guidelines.

The only two he followed were: 1. don't sweat the small stuff and 2. everything is small stuff.

Murphy was born knowing the meaning of life: eat when food is presented; sleep when you are bored; play with your pet at every opportunity and mark every bush within sight.

Were You There?
Vietnam Notes

"*Were You There?* reflects a deep under-standing of war, those who go to fight and their families. This understanding reaches beyond the Vietnam experience to soldiers and families of now."

Lee Gentry, former unit commander 11th armored Calvary regiment, Vietnam 1966-67.

Illumination Rounds

Illumination Rounds presents a graphic portrayal of American Soldiers and Marines in Vietnam.

Collectively, the stories present a captivating before, during and after picture of the men who fought.

The authors styles and recollections complement each other to capture the tragedy, humor, and perspective of the young men in that controversial conflict.

Color Me History

The author composed this coloring book for his granddaughters and for all beginning historians who enjoy adding color to life as well as parent librarians who keep their enthusiasm alive.

Coloring is fun! History is fun! Color more than 40 drawings and learn about historical people, places, and events in Saint Augustine. The city was founded in 1565 and is now more than 450 years old!